WARRIOR'S REVENGE

BY SHERRY ROBERTS

Warrior's Revenge
Down Dog Diary
Book of Mercy
Maud's House
Write Tips

WARRIOR'S REVENGE

A Novel by
SHERRY ROBERTS

Osmyrrah Publishing | Apple Valley, Minnesota

Osmyrrah Publishing
Apple Valley, Minnesota 55124
www.osmyrrahpublishing.com
info@osmyrrahpublishing.com

ISBN: 978-0-9638880-8-2

Library of Congress Control Number: 2016904965

Printed in the United States of America
First Edition

Cover Digital Art by Kathey Amaral: designbykatt.deviantart.com
Cover Photograph by Cathleen Tarawhiti: www.facebook.com/pages/
Cathleen-Tarawhiti-Photographer/95878166172
Model: Monique Wanner
Cover Church Photograph: Greg Mimbs, Mimbs Photography

TO CONNIE AND GEANETTE, WHO TAUGHT ME
THERE IS GRACE AND LOVE EVEN IN LOSS.

CHAPTER 1

MOURNING SHOES

O N THE DAY PETER Jorn saw a ghost, shoes fell from the sky.

Cheap sandals, worn Doc Martins, ratty house slippers, dirty tennis shoes—lots of tennis shoes. "She's crazy, always has been. Now she's flinging shoes from the roof," said the man next to me, a neighbor of the shoe tosser. Jorn and I were standing in a gathering crowd on the sidewalk in front of a group of brownstone apartments a block from the Minneapolis Institute of Art.

Watching from below as the police tried to calm the sobbing woman on the rooftop and disarm her of a particularly lethal-looking work boot, I asked the man, "Why is she doing this?"

"Lovers' breakup," he shrugged, as if love was no big deal even when it caused footwear to tumble from the heavens.

A woman in unflattering shorts and flip-flops, his wife perhaps, leaned around him and said, "Well, can you blame her? Breaking up by text."

"Really?" I said, enjoying this treat of insider information but also horrified at such a tacky ending to a relationship.

Jorn, not the type to appreciate a tasty morsel of gossip, tugged on my arm. "Let's go."

My informant and I traded grins, then she lifted a shoulder philosophically and imparted a final piece of wisdom, "Love can unhinge us all."

With one last glance toward the distraught woman being hustled off the roof by two police officers, Jorn and I walked to the museum. It was one-too-many-days-above-ninety-degrees in July, and it felt sublime to step inside the museum. Out of the heat and humidity that pressured us like an unseen but heavy hand, I wanted to wrap my arms around the tall, cool columns or lie down on the tile floors in a yoga Corpse Pose.

The calm of museums speaks to me, and the energies of creation fill me. I am truly my mother's daughter. Evie, an artist, has dragged me to museums since before I could walk. She told me I saw my first Monet while swaddled in a sling strapped across her chest.

The exhibit I came to see this day was called "The Mourners: Tomb Sculptures from the Court of Burgundy." When I asked Jorn to go with me, he said, "This isn't some modern crap, is it?"

"Modern?"

"Like someone leaning a bag of cat litter against the wall and calling it art."

"These are masterpieces from medieval tombs."

"Oh, well, that's *so* much better."

The Mourners are alabaster sculptures, ranging in height from ten to sixteen inches, all carved in various poses of grief. They were commissioned for the tomb of John the Fearless, whose nickname indicated his preference for battle over diplomacy. No stranger to the art of murder, John was ruthless in his pursuit of power and was himself assassinated on a bridge in 1419.

The four dukes of Burgundy, of which John the Fearless was one, loved luxury as much as they thirsted for power—which led them to commission art like what we saw before us, art timeless enough to travel through the centuries to a museum in Minneapolis. The exhibit occupied most of the wide hall on the museum's second floor, and the large Sunday crowd stood two and three deep against the ropes protecting a long table. On the table were dozens of exquisitely rendered poses of medieval devotion—a procession of monks wringing hands, deacons drying tears, and bishops in solemn contemplation. The detail of the work blew me away; the artists had brought rock to life. "Incredible, isn't it?" I said, admiring Mourner Number 78, his cowl hiding his shadowed face, his hand clutching a book painted red and gold.

"Yeah, that's something, all right," Jorn mumbled.

Jorn wasn't paying attention to me. He was studying something or someone across the hall. I raised my head to see what had captured his interest—and the next thing I knew Jorn was sprinting through the Asia exhibit. Of course, I had to follow.

Jorn appeared to have his sights on a tall man who was weaving in and out of the crowd, passing from one room to another. His stride was long and brisk. Wearing a hoodie, ragged jeans, and sandals, he could have been any of the art students I saw here regularly. At one point, he looked back, discovered Jorn still following him, and stepped up the pace. That brief glance didn't tell me much. A hood pulled low, like Mourner Number 78's, obscured his face, but I managed a glimpse of a black dreadlock whipping out from the hoodie's edge.

We lost him in Africa then heard sandals slapping on the marble stairs. He had doubled back to the Mourners in the main gallery and was climbing to the third floor. As we raced up after him, I heard Jorn groan. He had begun to limp. His war wound was acting up. As his yoga teacher, I should have said something, but the look on his face stopped me.

My name is Maya Skye, and I teach yoga to people seeking inner peace and to people like Jorn whose peace has been shattered. A journalist, Jorn is a foreign correspondent trapped by doctor's orders on domestic soil. In our short and sometimes prickly friendship, we've faced killers together and built a trust that thought nothing of careening around corners of valuable art together. We're civil (most of the time), supportive (all of the time), and good about keeping each other out of the soup. If Jorn was interested in the fellow we were pursuing, so was I.

Hoodie rounded the corner into European art, and Jorn's gait increased to a fast shuffle. We cut down a parallel hall, hoping to trap the man, but one of the guards busted us, "No running in the museum." We nodded, did a fast walk out of sight, then picked up the pace again. Where was the guy? The maze of exhibit rooms, hallways, and alcoves was defeating us. We'd lost him. We made a loop of the third floor—from Van Gogh's olive trees in Impressionism to some weird rooster sculpture in Folk Art and back again. Somehow Hoodie had slipped past us.

Pausing on a landing in the middle of the museum's marble staircase, we scanned the crowd gathered around the Mourners below and fought to regain our breath. Jorn leaned over and massaged his thigh.

"You know that guy?" I asked.

Jorn nodded. "You could say that."

He straightened and looked at me. "I killed him."

CHAPTER 2

A SIMPLE LOVE STORY

W E DROVE HOME TO Gabriel's Garden in silence. Gabriel's Garden is a small town about an hour outside of Minneapolis. If we had a museum, people wouldn't chase men through it. We are a quiet people, hunkered in front of our screens reading the online newspaper Jorn writes and edits. Everyone in town has a computer because my tech-obsessed, millionaire father gave one to each household. We have a high Google per capita rate, but sometimes not even all the information in the world can help a person understand the human heart. Often, it just takes plain old nosiness.

As my tailbone absorbed another bump on Interstate 94 courtesy of Jorn's decrepit Jeep, I tried to get him to talk.

"Tell me about the guy in the museum," I said. Nothing. I'd elicited more from Tibetan monks who'd sworn a vow of silence.

As he drove, Jorn stroked the scar at his temple and muttered to himself, always the same word.

Gasquet.

He repeated it over and over until it stopped sounding like a name and became little more than a string of nonsense sounds: gas-kay-gas-kay-gas-kay.

Jorn doesn't believe in vibes, but I can sense energies around people or in places. I knew Jorn was in a bad state right now.

I considered his admission of guilt in the museum. James Tumblethorne, my old friend, used to say guilt was an anchor on the heart. In a voice worn to a rasp by too much bar smoke and cheap whiskey, he would growl, "Guilt keeps you from moving on, from feeling the wind in your face. Let it go. What's done is done, kid." This was the advice of a former Hells Angel turned shaman.

But I knew it was never done.

Gasquet Dubois had been a photographer and Jorn's partner on numerous freelance assignments. They'd worked together for years, wrenching each other from scrapes in one hot spot after another—until the last one. Jorn had come back from that last assignment in Afghanistan, wounded. Gasquet had not come back at all, or so Jorn thought, until today.

THE NEXT DAY, I was surprised when Jorn walked into the Monday afternoon class at Breathe, my yoga studio. I thought, by the way he'd clammed up yesterday, that he would skip class and avoid me. Maybe he was ready to tell me the story of Gasquet the Ghost. He settled on one of the studio's mats positioned in the back of the room, his usual spot.

The class was full of regulars, about ten in all, and, like schoolchildren, each had his or her preferred place in the studio—smiling in front, hiding in back, blending in the middle. Today I was teaching standing poses to develop strength: the three Warrior Poses. The Warriors, however, are difficult, so while the class practiced these poses, I told them a love story to help them visualize the series.

"Once upon a time, there was a girl named Sati. She fell in love with and married a guy named Shiva. Shiva was quite a catch, being the lord of universal consciousness and all, but still Sati's father, a powerful king himself, was not happy with the marriage. So the king threw a big party and invited everyone but Shiva. Shiva didn't care; he was happy just sitting on his mountain, meditating. Sati, however, was incensed by the snub of her husband. In fact, she got so mad she burst into flames at the party."

"Ouch," said Olivia Chen, a fifteen-year-old kleptomaniac who changed hair color nearly as often as she changed her socks. "What a drama queen." She peeked over her arm stretched to the sky in Warrior and shared a smile with Tessa, the girl on the mat beside her. Olivia had begun bringing Tessa to yoga a few weeks ago. Where the petite Olivia was in constant motion like a hummingbird, lanky Tessa was a study in stillness, moving with the stealth of an egret stalking lunch. While Olivia would have chosen a location up front in class, she deferred to Tessa, who selected an inconspicuous spot in the middle of the flock.

I went on: "Devastated at the loss of Sati, the furious Shiva plucked out one of his dreadlocks and threw it down to the earth to create a demon warrior. Shiva sent the warrior to the party with instructions to cut off the king's head and put it on a pike so all could see the wrath of Shiva."

"Geez, Maya, I thought yoga was supposed to be non-violent," said Roselyn, wiping the sweat from her nose with a forearm speckled with paint. A middle school art teacher known as the Blue Lady, Roselyn loved the color blue so much that she immersed herself in it: in every room of her house, in the clothes she wore, in her periwinkle toenail polish and her turquoise yoga mat.

"Well, I think it's romantic, in a gory way," said Julia Lune, her arms beginning to wobble above her head. Julia was the town's celebrity romance writer.

Jorn grunted as he held his injured shoulder in Warrior II, a pose that requires patience and strength from all four limbs. "Cut to the chase, Maya."

"Relax," I said, and sighs echoed through the room. I demonstrated the flow again linking the three Warriors. I lunged forward with the right leg, lifting both arms straight up and arching my back. "Warrior I is the demon warrior sprouting from the earth to do Shiva's bidding." Keeping the front leg bent and the back leg straight, I opened my body to the side and extended my arms from the shoulders, one pointing ahead and one pointing behind. "In Warrior II," I told the class, "the warrior takes out his swords." Finally, I stepped into a T-shape, balancing on one leg, bending at the waist with both arms reaching out before me and one leg stretched out behind me. "In Warrior III, the warrior sets the king's head on the pike."

"Yuck," Olivia said, falling out of her Warrior then breaking into giggles. Tessa laughed with her but kept her balance. Olivia's friend had a quiet intensity about her; she observed everyone in class and learned quickly. She was always kind and helpful to Olivia, who was easily bored. Since Tessa came into klepto Olivia's life, fewer pens had disappeared from my studio.

"Of course, in yoga, there can be many meanings," I said, aiming a look at Jorn.

"Here it comes," said Jorn, easing out of his Warrior and rubbing his shoulder.

"In Warrior II, for example," I said, "we reach with courage toward the future with our arm pointing forward, while we recognize our connection to the past with the arm pointing behind us."

"I hope my future has chocolate cream pie in it," said Roselyn. I stepped over to Roselyn and placed a light hand on her shoulder helping her find the correct balance over her hips. I did this a lot during class, moving around the room from student to student, adjusting postures and whispering encouragement.

"Chocolate cream pie," Julia said with lust in her voice and dropping her arms.

As I sent Julia a smile, an angry voice disrupted class: "Tessa!"

Heads turned. Standing in the doorway to the studio

was a boy-man, about twenty, with close-cropped brown hair, corded arms, and filthy jeans and boots. He stomped across the polished oak floor to Tessa's mat. While everyone else had stopped and turned their attention to our intruder, Tessa had maintained her Warrior Pose. I glanced at Olivia, who looked worried. She had taken a step back and was nervously twisting a pink braid between her fingers.

Tessa kept her T-shape in Warrior III right up to the moment when the man yanked her out of it.

"Hey!" I shouted.

Jorn and I were across the room before either of us gave it a thought. I was about to grab the guy when he released Tessa and swung around to confront me. He was tall, strong, and trouble. He carried an unsettling energy—dark and bottled. I glanced from the man vibrating with anger to Tessa, who was warily watching him.

"Who are you?" I demanded.

He looked me up and down. I relaxed my shoulders. If he thought that display of ignorant testosterone was going to intimidate me, he was mistaken. Stepping in to diffuse the palpable tension, Tessa said, "This is Valmer, my brother."

"I'm Tessa's yoga teacher," I said to Valmer. "And I don't appreciate people barging into my class."

The man turned away, dismissing me. "Let's go," he said to his sister.

"Tessa, you can finish the class," I said.

Valmer ignored me.

Instead, he pointed at Tessa. "You know Pa wouldn't like this—this Satan stuff." He gave his sister a look that she obviously understood. With a nod, she crouched and began rolling up her yoga mat, one of the extras I kept for walk-ins.

As she rolled the mat, her brother continued to berate her. "This girly is going to fill your head with heathen." He swept his arm out, motioning toward the table at the front of the room behind my yoga mat. On the table was a Buddha statue and several lit candles. "Then Pa will really have to straighten you out. You're lucky I'm here and not him."

As a student of yoga, I had come up against the prejudice of religion before, so Valmer's attitude didn't surprise me. Maybe I was a heathen, but I definitely was *not* a "girly." I itched to set Valmer straight but felt Jorn's restraining hand on my arm. He was right. Nothing could be gained getting into a philosophical discussion with Valmer. I looked at Tessa, who was standing quietly beside her brother. I was puzzled by her energy—it wasn't fear exactly, more like regret.

Finally, Tessa's brother turned and marched from the room. Without a word, Tessa followed him. Just as she reached the door, I said loud enough for both to hear: "*Namaste*, Tessa."

Although she didn't look back, Tessa's step faltered slightly. Then the door to Breathe slammed, and the tension in the class shattered.

ON A CALM DAY, Olivia Chen was often moving something—jiggling a leg, playing with her hair, texting invisible messages on any nearby surface. So, after the episode with Tessa's brother, she was an orchestra of twitching. I cornered her after class, sat her down on my yoga mat, and tried to calm her.

"I hope Tessa's going to be okay," she whispered.

"I'm sure she'll be fine," I said, glancing over her head at Jorn, who had stayed behind and was now leaning against the brick wall of the studio, listening.

Olivia shook her shiny blue-black hair, its single pink braid catching on her cheek. She flicked the braid aside and continued tapping on her leg. "Her dad and brother are nuts. Her dad's super-religious, and her brother's ex-military."

"How do you know they're nuts?"

"Because Tessa told me. Her dad has that church out in the country and makes her go to service on Sunday—for HOURS."

"And the brother?"

"He works on a farm next door, and he *loves* guns."

Unease rippled through me. I had been raised in New Mexico, in a community of families dedicated to nonviolence. It was called Whispering Spirit Farm, and firearms of any kind were forbidden on commune property. I had never touched a gun. Evie hated them and had drummed into me that guns were weapons of convenience. She maintained, "It ought to take some work to snuff out a life, Maya."

I knew otherwise. Sometimes you can deal out death without even thinking or intending to; *sometimes killing is unbearably easy.*

"Val is a real douche bag," Olivia said. "He's bossy, thinks he knows everything just because he was a soldier. And he doesn't like Asians."

"What?"

"He calls me Fortune Cookie." Olivia's voice changed, deepened, nailing Val's lazy drawl. "Jerk. I'm as American as he is and, like, a million times smarter."

It was true. The daughter of two busy research scientists at the University of Minnesota, Olivia probably tested off the charts. Her body raced and so did her mind. Olivia's parents hoped yoga would plant the seed of calm in their daughter and, as Mrs. Chen said, "keep her off the streets and out of gangs." Mrs. Chen had learned all about gangs from American television.

After Olivia left, I invited Jorn up to my apartment for a glass of lemonade. I live in an old fire station. The first floor, where the town's fire engine used to be housed, is my studio. The second floor, where firemen once played cards, napped on the sofas, and cooked spaghetti in the kitchen, is my home. A spiral staircase connects the studio to my apartment. I have one bedroom and an open area that I have divided into living room and kitchen with bright rugs and strategic furniture arrangement—a tactic my orderly sister, Heart, had seen in an old *Martha Stewart Living* magazine.

Making himself at home on my red sofa, Jorn said, "Don't get involved in that girl's problems, Maya."

"Somebody has to help her."

"Did Tessa ask for your help?" Jorn sipped his lemonade. Leave it to him to bring the practical into all of this. "You could make it worse for her. She's tough. She knows how to handle her brother and father. She's been doing it for a long time."

"That's what I'm afraid of," I said. "Do you know her father?"

"I've seen him around. The Reverend Harold Miley. He emails me the schedule of services for his church each month to post in the newspaper." Jorn is publisher of the local newspaper, *The Independent*.

"She's just a kid, Jorn."

"So's the brother, if I'm not mistaken. He can't be more than twenty-one and already has a tour of Afghanistan under his belt."

Val did have that look of interrupted childhood, of something irretrievably lost, a warrior too soon.

"He's a walking PTSD bomb," Jorn said. "Don't be anywhere around when he blows."

"Posttraumatic stress disorder?"

Jorn nodded. "Most definitely. He looked wired; I bet he has nightmares. And he was carrying. There was a gun tucked in the back of his pants."

I straightened in shock. "I didn't see that," I said. I pointed angrily to the door. "There is clearly a sign on this building: 'No Firearms Allowed'."

"I doubt Val reads signs."

This really steamed me. I had noticed the dark energy around Tessa's brother and thought it was just because he was a miserable human being. Now, I realized he was miserable, armed, and dangerous.

"If he comes back again—" I was interrupted by the ping of Jorn's phone. He took it out and tapped the message button. His face went white, and he sank back into the sofa.

"What is it?" My hand automatically reached out to him. He looked at me, and his expression scared me.

"Jorn?"

He slowly turned the phone in my direction. I caught my breath. It was a message from the late Gasquet Dubois. It said: *I am alive.*

CHAPTER 3

SEE HOW THEY FALL

I AM ALIVE.

At first, I felt joy for Jorn; his best friend had survived. But the more I thought about it, the phrasing bothered me. It sounded like a hand clawing up from the grave. A warning. Deep inside, I began to wonder: Was this a friendly greeting? While Jorn trusted facts before intuition, I always listened to my inner Spirit. Messages from dead men usually were not warm and fuzzy. They were creepy. Still, if it were true . . .

"This is great news," I said, "isn't it?"

"Yes, yes, of course," Jorn stammered absently.

I knew that look on his face, that tone of voice. Jorn's quick mind had leaped over the initial shock and already had begun tunneling for answers. The reporter's litany of who, what, where, when, why, and how was digging through painful memories, official reports, and past conversations.

Suddenly, he began typing on his phone. I leaned over his shoulder and read: *Where are you?*

We waited for a reply. None came.

While Jorn was silent, his tense body was doing plenty of talking. This I could help with. As a practitioner of reiki, I channel energy into the body to spark healing and spread well-being. I had given Jorn reiki many times since we met months ago. Not really trusting in alternative therapies, he always grumbled at first, but, eventually, gave in to the relief created by his torn body sucking healing energy from the universe via my hand. Today, he didn't even grumble. I knew he was in pain. I placed my hand on his singing hip, where the bullet had entered, and felt the tension. As my hand began to warm, he leaned his head back against the sofa, closed his eyes, and heaved a sigh of relief.

I said conversationally, "You can't announce you're a murderer, as you did yesterday, and not expect me to be a little curious. And now you're receiving text messages from a dead man."

Opening his eyes and rolling his head so his gaze met mine, he whispered, "It was Gasquet in the museum." His blue eyes turned confused, haunted. "But how can that be?"

"Tell me about Gasquet, about that last assignment."

Jorn hesitated. He made his living excavating other people's memories but did not like unearthing his own. After a while, though, he began to talk. "I made him go."

"Where?"

"Up into the mountains. To meet Faud, a tribal leader."

18

"For a story?"

"A follow-up to our series on child soldiers in Africa. Most people don't realize it's a problem in Afghanistan and other Middle Eastern countries, too. Most of Faud's soldiers could neither read nor write. Half of them were barely as tall as the guns they carried." I was not surprised to hear disgust in Jorn's tone. I'd read some of his old articles online. He had a soft spot for the underdog, the abused, the violated. We had that in common.

"I wanted that story. But Gasquet had a bad feeling about it from the start. I teased him. He was a superstitious cuss. Never took off that Saint Joseph medal of his."

Jorn reached into his pocket and pulled out an oval-shaped medal on a chain: Saint Joseph, the patron saint of families and the home. He leaned forward, arms on knees, and rubbed the silver medal between his fingers. I kept my hand on his injured hip.

Jorn's voice softened. "It was an ambush. Faud's kids were waiting for us." Jorn's hand tightened around the medal. "Gasquet was driving. There was no place to hide on that goddamn mountain road."

I could imagine their helplessness. I'd been on such narrow mountain paths, the mountain soaring straight up one side and plummeting straight down the other. On those roads, mere ledges of transportation, you hung on for dear life, even during a casual drive. Jorn and Gasquet would have been easy targets for snipers hiding on higher ground. The only escape would have been down, over the side of the mountain.

I didn't want to hear the rest, but Jorn was back there, reliving the nightmare.

"When they hit . . . I told him to leave the damn cameras!" His voice changed, becoming rough with urgency. "We gotta get out of here, man! Jump, G! Jump!"

I didn't know what to say except "I'm sorry. So sorry."

He turned to me, watery eyes pleading for me to understand. "Our Jeep was no protection. No top. Hell, no doors. Completely exposed. I tried to get him out. I grabbed him and—"

From the way he was fingering the chain and medal, I could envision Jorn pulling at Gasquet, catching the necklace along with his shirt, holding on. Jorn would not have let go of his friend.

"Bullets were flying everywhere. The windshield shattered. I saw Gasquet get hit—once, twice." His words faded.

I waited.

"No time to think . . . No time . . . So I jumped . . . And I took Gasquet with me."

He sat back, his posture resigned. I imagined Jorn wrenching them both out of the Jeep, into the air, into a free fall over a mountain cliff. They would have become like rocks once they hit the ground, tumbling down, down, until they slammed into a tree and stopped. Between the bullet wounds and the rugged terrain, it was a wonder Jorn had survived.

The sadness of memories overcame Jorn, and he leaned against me, exhausted from dredging them up. The shoulder that had taken one bullet was heavy against mine. The head where another bullet had parted his long, sun-streaked hair was close to my cheek. My hand went back to the hip that would never be the same. Almost immediately, it was calling to me, radiating warmth.

We sat there, and evening fell. Bella the cat leaped up on the sofa and butted Jorn's arm. He absently stroked her head as she curled beside him. Bella's purr, so big for such a small thing, filled the room like the hum of a motor. After a while, I heard Jorn humming as well: "Lady Madonna."

Finally, Jorn leaned forward and reached for his lemonade with a trembling hand. He drank half the glass. When he straightened, he was rubbing Saint Joseph again. "We were singing that day," he said thoughtfully. "Gasquet can't carry a tune worth a damn, but he loves the Beatles." Jorn was piecing the incident together in his mind, going over every detail. How many times had he done this?

"I grabbed Gasquet. We fell through the air then hit the ground." Jorn's voice changed, and he was no longer talking to me. He was talking to Gasquet. "'Fuck, that hurt. Hey, man, you okay? We gotta get outa here.'"

He stopped. I held my breath, waiting, then he whispered, "I killed him when I dragged him into that ambush. I saw the bullet hole in his head. He was dead. I swear he was." Jorn touched the scar at his temple. "I don't know what happened next."

Then Jorn turned to me, a stricken look on his face. "Did I leave him *alive* on that mountain? Did I leave Gasquet to the Taliban?"

EXHAUSTED, JORN SPENT THE night on the sofa, wrapped in my arms, Bella draped over his leg.

I didn't sleep much. My mind went back to years ago, to my first days in the ashram in India. I'd run to Guru Bob, fleeing from events in a New York alley. My spirit was shattered. I was so lost I couldn't even figure out how to get out of bed or eat or pray. All I could think about was: I'd killed a man in that alley. My mother said it was an accident. My father called it self-defense. My spirit, however, knew it was unforgivable.

At the ashram, Guru Bob passed no judgment, made no excuses. When I told him my story, he sat for a long time in silence, his legs crossed on a prayer rug, white robes resembling meringue all around him. He wore a New York Yankees baseball cap firmly on his bald head.

Finally, he looked at me with those penetrating eyes and said, "Man, hard to come back from that."

I nearly fell off my prayer mat. Where were the words of wisdom I had traveled thousands of miles to hear?

"How do I make amends?" I asked Guru Bob. "How do I find forgiveness?"

"Is that why you're here?"

"Yes."

"You think I hand out forgiveness like lollipops?"

My heart fell. This would not be easy. I asked in a quiet voice, "Maybe you could show me the way?"

"Do I look like a tour guide?" Guru Bob could be tough love incarnate.

Perturbed, I said, "Frankly, yes. You *are* a guru."

Guru Bob puffed, a piffle sound. "There is no trying, no path to forgiveness, Maya."

This was not what I wanted to hear. I wanted some penance, some Twelve Steps, some way to wipe the slate clean—and told Guru Bob so.

"Maya, Maya," he said, with an understanding smile on his face, "forgiveness is not something you do. It is something you are."

Beside me, Jorn mumbled in his sleep and I leaned closer. He said, "I gotta find him." He was talking about Gasquet.

"I'll help you," I whispered.

CHAPTER 4

COWBOYS AND HEROES

PETER JORN'S HOUSE MIRRORS its owner—comfortably messy. Just as I knew that Jorn was likely wearing two socks of different colors and probably hadn't combed his hair yet today, I knew that his living room with its piles of books and stacks of newspapers as high as end tables disguised a delightfully cozy place to spend an evening, once you uncovered a chair or two. Jorn owned two leather Mission chairs and matching ottomans; a seldom-used fat old TV in the corner; floor lamps, which he typically left on all the time; and weeks' worth of the *New York Times* and *The Wall Street Journal*. I could hear my father, Larry, complaining, "Cripes, he couldn't save a few million trees and subscribe online?"

Jorn's need to surround himself with yellowing newspaper, despite being the publisher of an online publication, was so old school.

Still, this homey chaos suited Jorn as did the pristine and tidy condition of his kitchen. I had discovered, much to my pleasure, that Jorn loved to cook. Watching him mix a vinaigrette—from scratch—I had to admit he looked good amid his top-of-the-line coffee maker and expensive pots and pans dangling from a rack over the butcher block island.

While Jorn found relaxation, even solace, in cooking, I tackled the stove for the sake of nourishment only. To be frank, cooking bored me, and Jorn knew it. That's why I usually filled the role of pack horse.

As I stepped out the back door onto Jorn's deck, I juggled a tray piled with plates, buns, cutlery, and condiments. Jorn had already brought out the salad and was now commanding the grill, which was not some weenie hibachi. Sitting with a beer and watching Jorn impose his will on fire and sausages was not a bad way to spend a golden summer evening in Gabriel's Garden. Such Minnesota evenings are supposed to make us forget that last brutal winter, and they nearly always do. Everyone wants to be out in these long twilights: the kids playing ball on the field down the street, the couples strolling hand in hand or pushing heavy-duty strollers down Maple Lane, the runners taking one last spin around Lake Michael a few blocks away.

"Thank God, you're not a vegetarian," Jorn said in a tone that made healthy living sound like a crime.

I handed him a beer. "Make mine extra crispy."

"That's the only way I cook."

Leaning to dodge the smoke, I told him that my father had tried to trace Gasquet's message.

He paused with tongs lifted in the air then went back to turning the sausages. "Burner phone, I bet."

Larry, the wizard behind the tech curtain in my life, said prepaid phones are cheap and untraceable. They make excellent tools for organizing revolutions or sending mysterious messages.

"Actually, it wasn't a burner," I said. "The text came from Gasquet's phone."

That jolted Jorn. He swung toward me, nearly sliding the brats off the plate. Carefully, he turned back, lowered the lid on the grill, and sat down at the table. "He's sure?"

I gave him a look and stabbed a blackened brat. He passed me the salad and said, "Of course, he's sure." Jorn knew my father's incomparable capabilities when it came to ferreting out information from the cyber world.

"Larry tried tracking the phone, but it was disabled as soon as the message was sent."

Jorn thumped the bottom of the ketchup bottle to get the ketchup moving. "None of it makes sense. Not the message, not the sighting at the museum."

"It's all rather dramatic," I said, breaking the skin of the brat and tasting the smoky flavor. "Maybe it's somebody impersonating Gasquet."

"How did they get Gasquet's phone and who was the guy at the museum?" Jorn picked at his salad and recalled his friend. "Gasquet was goofy and—French. He told corny jokes and thought they were outrageously funny. He didn't get along with his father, but then a lot of people rebel against their dads." Jorn took a long pull from his beer. "I don't know what to believe. I thought he was dead. My God, if I left him there—"

"Was his body ever brought home?" I asked.

"Not that I could find. When I got out of the hospital, I checked with the Red Cross and my military contacts. No one knew anything about a photographer having been killed in that area. Since I got the text message, I've called all my old contacts again, talked to the editors we worked for. Still nothing. No one has heard from Gasquet in months."

"Did you tell them he was dead?"

"No."

I knew why Jorn hadn't been more forthcoming with his editors. The text message had lit a tinder of hope in him that perhaps his friend was still alive. "Gasquet called us cowboys. We went where the story took us. We sang Beatles songs on back roads and shared crappy meals over campfires." He finished one brat and reached for another one. "This doesn't sound like Gasquet, but he *was* a prankster. He just might use some old B-horror movie line. He would think it was funny."

"What do you think he's up to?"

Jorn paused, ketchup bottle in hand. "I don't know. This is just not like him. But after months behind enemy lines?" He looked thoughtfully out into the woods that bordered his backyard. I followed his gaze. Darkness was coming, working its way through the cottonwoods and oaks, dismissing the softness of the evening. The streets and ball field had grown quiet. The mosquitoes soon would be upon us.

Jorn turned back to his meal, absently slapping at the

first of our blood-thirsty visitors. I was not so care-free. Minnesota's Unofficial State Bird, as our mosquitoes are often called, present an ethical issue for me. I attract the pesky bloodsuckers like a magnet. They test my commitment to *ahimsa*, the yogic principle of harming no living thing.

"I've been thinking," Jorn said. "I need to talk to Gasquet's family. I know there was a rift, but maybe he's contacted them. All this mystery—the message and the museum—it's just not like Gasquet. I'm beginning to wonder if I knew him at all."

Until now, Jorn had painted a sunny picture of Gasquet, but shadows had begun to creep in. Instead of placing a comforting hand on Jorn's arm as I wanted to, I softly flicked away a mosquito feasting on his cheek.

JORN WANTED TO SEE the security tapes from the day we visited "The Mourners" exhibit. After I had explained to Evie about the incident at the Minneapolis Institute of Art and the strange text message Jorn had received, Evie had made a quick call to the museum and announced, "No problem."

The chief of security, an ex-cop who drew himself up like a bantam rooster, wasn't happy about showing us the security tape. He was quite clear: he did not approve, even if my mother was good friends with the museum board and a generous donor.

We arrived at the museum on Wednesday morning just as it was opening its doors. In minutes, Jorn, the security chief, and I were peering over the shoulder of a computer guy running the tape from three days ago. "There!" I pointed to a figure on the screen. We all leaned closer. It was the mystery man all right—bundled in a black hoodie on a miserably hot day. The technician tapped at the keyboard, switching back and forth between cameras, and we were able to follow the man as he wandered the galleries of the museum.

"Does he move like Gasquet?" I questioned Jorn.

Jorn studied the screen. "Yes. It's him."

I refrained from pointing out that we still hadn't gotten a clear visual of his face.

The man Jorn was calling Gasquet spent a long time in Impressionism, gave Modern and Contemporary barely a glance, and then settled in Baroque. He sat on a bench in front of a contemporary painting that was far different from the other paintings in this room of seventeenth-century European art. He studied the painting for exactly eighteen minutes, looked at his watch, and then walked to the long hall where the Mourners were on display. He circled the exhibit, sliding in and out of the crowd, until he finally took up a position directly opposite Jorn. There, he leaned against a column and waited.

He alternated between studying the Mourners and studying Jorn, always keeping his face angled away from the security cameras. We never got a good look at his face, just a tip of a dark bronze chin and a glimpse of dreadlock. He kept his hands tucked in his pockets.

"That's when I noticed him," Jorn said as the man on the monitor whirled and disappeared into one of the nearby galleries. On the monitors, I watched us chase the figure in and out of one gallery after another. I saw when Jorn started to limp, our run-in with the guard, and the annoyance on Jorn's face when we lost the hooded figure.

"Where did he go?" I asked. "How did he leave?"

The computer guy clicked across the keyboard and pulled up another image. "He walked out the front door, cool as you please."

I sighed. "And we never saw his face."

"It doesn't matter," said Jorn. "It was Gasquet."

I know what Jorn thought he saw, but I wasn't sold. We never got a good look at the man, a positive ID.

"I don't know who this fella is," the security chief said with a satisfied grin, "but he sure led you on a merry chase."

I ignored the barb. "Jorn, how did he know you would be at the museum on Sunday?"

Jorn was baffled. "Hell if I know."

"Are we finished playing amateur detective now?" asked the security chief.

Not able to think of anything else we could gain from the security footage, I reluctantly said yes, and he escorted us to the door of the security office.

Before leaving the museum, we stopped by the Baroque Gallery to see the painting that had held such appeal for Gasquet the Mystery Man. Jorn and I sat on the bench where Gasquet had sat. We stared at the massive painting in front of us: *Santos-Dumont—The Father of Aviation II* by Kehinde Wiley. Wiley was known for his large-scale paintings of young black men depicted in the tradition of "old master" canvases—posed as kings, saints, men of importance and power. This twenty-first-century painting had drawn some controversy for its placement in the Baroque Gallery, but I liked it here. It was a fresh breeze with underlying tones of Old World drama.

In the painting, two men have fallen from the sky and landed on a rocky outcrop. For models, the artist had chosen young men from the slums of Rio de Janeiro and dressed them in contemporary clothing: T-shirts and lightweight pants. They couldn't be more different from Alberto Santos-Dumont, considered the Father of Aviation in Brazil. He had been white, the heir of a rich Brazilian family, well-known for his airship flights, and the first to achieve flight of a powered airplane. I couldn't take my eyes from the painting or get the title out of my mind. Kids from the ghetto depicted as pioneers, as imaginations that had taken flight and suffered, as adventurers who had seen what the rest of us couldn't yet see. It was magnificent, but . . .

"Why this painting?" I wondered.

After studying the painting for several moments, Jorn whispered, "They're fallen heroes."

Did the mystery man consider Gasquet and Jorn fallen heroes? After all, they had sacrificed to bring the world the truth through their words and pictures and been struck down. I kept that thought to myself, however. Although I had certainly seen him perform some heroics, Jorn would not like to be called a hero.

We stayed for a long time in that quiet room, not talking, just sitting with *Santos-Dumont*.

As we left, I gave the security camera a little wave.

CHAPTER 5

ROCKING THE CHAPEL OF THE FORGIVING HEART

I WONDERED WHAT PETER JORN had been like before he was betrayed by a tribal leader, shot by child soldiers, and left for dead. So, I asked if he had a photo of him and Gasquet. With a nod, he rummaged through the disaster area he called a desk, pulled out a photograph, and handed it to me.

This was a Jorn I'd never seen. He and Gasquet were smiling straight into the camera, arms around each other's shoulders. They looked so young, so happy, so free. Their drab desert jackets appeared dusty, and each had a checkered scarf wrapped around his neck. In the background were unforgiving mountains. The men looked as if it had been a long time between the indulgences of civilization and they didn't mind. It was obvious at first glance—they were brothers, in sweat and spirit.

Their looks couldn't have been more different. My sister, Heart, once said Jorn reminded her of a young Robert Redford—not the clean-cut lawyer who danced on a New York rooftop for Jane Fonda but the scrappy Sundance Kid leaping off the cliff with Butch Cassidy. He looked especially so in this photo, with longish sun-streaked hair, a scruffy blond mustache (now gone), and a devil-may-care gleam in his eyes (still there but no so frequent since his experiences in Afghanistan).

Gasquet Dubois's face—smooth, bronzed, and wreathed with dark brown dreadlocks—held a serenity, a patience that balanced Jorn's alacrity. His smile, bracketed by puckish dimples, said he enjoyed laughing and he'd follow Jorn anywhere. While Jorn would plunge without a thought into the deep for a story, Gasquet would be the one to warn of monsters, then shake his head as if to say "what can you do?" and dive in after him.

I took a photo of the photo with my smartphone.

As I drove to Evie's house, I couldn't get Gasquet's image out of my mind. He was lit from within with a joy for life, his smile so empty of hate that it almost hurt my heart. I had met people like him. Their presence both filled me with beauty and worried me. They were gifts that the world seldom appreciated; too often they were seen as weak and thus dispensable. I wanted to meet Gasquet just for his smile alone.

I pulled up in front of my parents' house, a stone octagonal structure designed by Evie and an homage to her love of sacred mathematics. Filled with Evie's calm energy and Larry's cyber excitement, it was a healing place. I always felt lighter when I crossed its threshold. I rapped once on the front door and let myself in. Following the smell of paint and mineral spirits, I entered Evie's studio, a bright room overlooking her riotous garden in the backyard. Encased in one of Larry's old flannel shirts and speckled with paint from her fingertips to her elbows, Evie smiled and offered her cheek for me to kiss. I did just that and stepped back to examine her work in progress: a painting of huge white peonies. It would have been a pleasant floral still life, except for the rabbit. With heavy heads bending low, and ominously, the gang of blooms circled a wide-eyed baby rabbit. Was the rabbit hiding or were the flowers hungry?

It could go either way, knowing Evie. Today I decided to go with the dark side. "Carnivorous peonies." I wiggled an eyebrow. "I like it. But poor bunny."

Evie tilted her head. "Oh, I think he'll get out of it. I've left the slightest hole."

I searched for the escape hatch, and there it was. Evie's art was never comfortable and never mean. It displayed a dark corner in my mother that we seldom saw in daily living but which I was happy existed. It comforted me to know that my mother wasn't calm and even-tempered all the way through, that there was a rebel secreted within her. Though she had lived many years in a commune, my mother was not a true Earth Mother type. No limp dresses and sandals for her. She preferred penny loafers, even in summer, and slim trousers and simple shirts. But she did carry that ambiance of contentment I came to take for granted in many of the women at Whispering Spirit Farm. A trait I envied.

"I don't mean to interrupt," I said.

Without even knowing what I wanted, she already had turned toward her paint-spattered table of jars, brushes, and tubes of paint and begun to clean up. Wrapping her brush in newspaper to squeeze out the excess paint, she asked, "Where are we going?"

"On an adventure."

That was all Evie needed to know.

I liked driving at this time of day, with the windows down and the dusky sounds and grassy smells filling the car. In the golden light, the fields of corn and sunflowers seemed at rest. They rolled away from the road as far as the eye could see. Now, they were green and hopeful and young. By August, the corn would be tall and the yellow sunflower heads would be heavy.

About ten miles out of town, I turned onto a country road. Evie asked, "Did you find what you were looking for at the museum?"

"Jorn is sure it was Gasquet, more than ever, but I have my doubts."

She shrugged. "The human mind will see what it wants to see, even in the dark."

I glanced at Evie. "I mean, I want it to be Gasquet. I want Jorn to get his friend back, but—"

"Your intuition is telling you there's something fishy going on."

"Yes. That's why I need the diary," I said.

I felt Evie shift toward me. "Are you sure?"

The Down Dog Diary, as we kids at Whispering Spirit Farm always called it, is the mysterious journal of my old friend and mentor James Tumblethorne. He was a shaman and the last of a long line of protectors of the diary. For a hundred years, shamans have recorded daily ramblings, stories, warnings, and morsels of wisdom in the journal. When Tum was killed, I inherited the diary. I am its current keeper, but I don't exactly know what that job entails or where the diary is at the moment.

Tum was murdered by people who believed the diary held the secret of immortality. As Jorn would say, some people will believe anything. But when they came after me to get the diary and Jorn was caught in the crossfire, I decided it was too dangerous to keep the diary around my family. So, I arranged for it to go into hiding: I gave it to my father. Larry is good at making things disappear.

"You think the diary will help you find Gasquet?" Evie asked.

"I don't know." It is difficult to explain how holding the diary, thumbing through its pages, and reading random passages makes me feel stronger and less alone in my new calling. I have missed that feeling since I entrusted the book to Larry. The entire time it has been tucked away in a safe nest of Larry's making, I have felt a yearning for it. I am connected to it somehow, now. I want to open the diary and be embraced by its smells. That's what's funny about the diary. Only the keeper can smell the different aromas that lift from its pages, and these fragrances or odors are always changing: from nose-wrinkling moldy cardboard to the wholesome scent of a baby's chubby neck. Jorn and I had fought the men who came after the diary and won—but not without cost. Jorn had been wounded, and I had added another blot to my karmic scorecard.

"If you need it, you need it," Evie said. "Your father will just have to find a new hiding place when you're finished with the diary."

"I know. I hope he won't be too upset."

"He'll love it."

I agreed and took a deep breath of satisfaction. It felt good to have made the decision about the diary and to be sharing the evening with Evie. When a breeze lifted Evie's short gray-streaked hair, I spotted a few strands of green where she'd run paint-smeared fingers through it. My mother had a way of closing her eyes, lifting her nose like a deer testing the air, and taking in the peace of a moment; she was doing it now. Without opening her eyes, she asked, "So, what is my role on this field trip?"

My mother always knew when I had an agenda. Heart and I are convinced that Evie has x-ray vision into our souls.

"We're visiting the Reverend Harold Miley," I said.

Evie searched her memory. "He has that evangelical church, doesn't he?"

"That's the one. His daughter was taking yoga—until recently."

Evie opened her eyes and looked at me. "I see."

I told Evie about Valmer's visit to Breathe. "I don't like him. He's a bully. And the father probably is, too."

"Maya, this is not a crusade you can win. Men like the Mileys don't change their minds."

"That's why you're here. No one can say no to you." My

mother has a calming effect over her surroundings and the people in it. I've seen her walk through a group of gang-bangers hassling everyone they met on the street—until they met Evie. Experiencing just a touch of her smile, they parted like the Red Sea for my mother. Larry once told me, "Your mother *is* peace. She can calm about anything, even wild dogs probably. I've seen her in action in many lifetimes." My parents believe this is not their first dance together on this earth.

Evie laughed and shook her head. "Maya, Maya. My fighter."

"Tessa's a good kid, Evie. She's like a sponge, taking in experiences through her pores. And yoga makes her happy; I can see it. She was born for the mat. She rides her bike into town to go to yoga, all the way from out here. Just stand around and do your thing, okay?"

"My thing," Evie pondered the farmland and the edge of woods growing closer as we drove.

"Generate the calm."

"What's the child's name?"

"Tessa."

"Tessa," she repeated softly, rolling it around in her mother's mind, and I relaxed. With that one word, I knew that Evie in her mysterious way had taken Tessa in.

I turned off the paved country road and onto a gravel one that led to a clapboard church with bright red doors. On the steeple, which was missing some shingles, was a waiting crow. I watched the crow as we slowly got out of the car. It cried out to us and dipped its head. I looked around for the reverend's house. Suddenly, the crow lifted into the air and streaked down a narrow lane behind the chapel. That must be where Tessa, her father, and her brother lived.

The church stood like a sentinel, woods thick with oak and pine behind it. On either side of the road to the church was pasture, which, from the look of the ruts, was used for Sunday parking. I peered into the crowding woods, and suddenly had the feeling someone was there, watching us. But the crow had given no serious warning, so I lowered my shoulders. If the bird was okay with what was out there, it couldn't be too bad, could it? Crows are intelligent and not easily taken in. I have a long history with crows and trust them.

"What a lovely church," Evie said, slamming the car door and taking a step. A simple wooden cross sat atop the red arched double doors, the shiny red paint glowing against the once-white, now-gray clapboards. On both sides of the church were small leaded windows, arched as well. Beside the front steps was a wooden sign: Chapel of the Forgiving Heart.

Evie looked around, and the smile slid from her face. "Oh shit," she said.

I swung toward her in shock. Evie never cursed; I was the potty mouth in the family. I immediately scanned the area for what could have disturbed Evie, but I saw nothing out of the ordinary. "What is it?"

She nodded at a second sign to the left of the front steps. The white canvas banner stretched between two poles said: "TENT REVIVAL. Aug 4–10. Praying, singing, witnessing, mini-donuts, and lemonade. All welcome."

I was confused. Why would a tent revival upset Evie? I

was about to ask her when the red doors of the old church burst open and out slid a man with all the theatrics of Tom Cruise in *Risky Business*. Gray-streaked, chin-length wavy hair swung in all directions, and the coattails of his dated suit, a secondhand black tux, whirled as he leapt down the steps, voice bellowing, arms sweeping through the air as if conducting an orchestra. When he noticed us, the smile on his face grew and he sang even louder, a tune of resurrection—"He's Alive" by Dolly Parton.

He circled us and the car on dancing feet, still singing and smiling. Evie smiled back. I followed him with my eyes. Even when he skipped behind me, I turned, keeping my gaze on the preacher.

And then he was finished. His arms dropped to his sides, and he bowed his head in prayer, or waiting for our applause. In contrast to serious Valmer, the preacher was a man possessed of good cheer, or maybe just possessed. I didn't know what to say to the Reverend Harold Miley.

"Sometimes you've just got to let the spirit soar, right?" the preacher asked, grinning from me to Evie. "Welcome, welcome to the Chapel of the Forgiving Heart. Where the lost are found, the desperate are comforted, the Lord blesses us all."

"And the soul sings," added Evie.

The Reverend Miley brightened. "Hey, I like that. Mind if I use it?"

"Not at all," said Evie. She was enjoying the minister.

I stepped forward and introduced Evie and myself. Val had obviously filled the minister in on me. "You own the yoga studio. I know the place. What can I do for you?"

Never patient with chit-chat, I said, "I want to talk about Tessa coming back to class."

Without a change in his pleasant expression, he swept his wavy hair back from his thin face and said, "Oh, I don't think so." The energy shifted around us as it does when you realize you are not just dealing with an immovable obstacle, but one that is steadfast and probably nuts. I felt Evie edge closer to me, but when I glanced at her, she was studying the minister with kind eyes.

"But she's learning so much," I said.

"That's the trouble. Tessa's always learning."

"Sounds like an intelligent girl," Evie said.

Grinning even more, the Reverend Miley leaned toward Evie. "She's got her mother's brains. God rest her soul."

"Then, surely, she's smart enough to see that yoga will not interfere with," Evie paused, glancing at the tent revival sign and back, "her spiritual life."

The Reverend Miley rocked on his heels. "Now, I don't know all that much about the benefits, or even purpose, of twisting the human body into shapes God never intended. Maybe you're all just having fun. But Val tells me there's an altar, a heathen idol, and candles. I can't hold with that."

"But Reverend—" I said.

"I got to protect my girl. Tessa was raised in the house of the Lord, and that's where she's staying." A stubborn look flashed across the preacher's face, gone as quickly as it had come. Suddenly, he shifted gears, a grin reappeared, and he lifted his arms as if to embrace the air. "What an evening."

He abruptly turned, tails flying, and started down the path around the side of the church. We'd been dismissed.

"*Namaste*, Reverend," I yelled. He didn't turn around.

"See you at the tent revival, ladies." His words floated up over his shoulder with a wave of his hand. "It's gonna be a humdinger."

Evie and I paused as we opened our car doors. Night sounds were revving up around the small church. Energies were at battle here, as they were in any house of worship. I was drawn to these energies, where pain and love, despair and joy, had soaked into the worn wooden pews and the scuffed floor. For someone who practices no codified religion, I'd found peace in many churches and spent hours in them. Still, I wondered, was the Chapel of the Forgiving Heart like one of Evie's paintings—lovely on the outside but with a darkness at the core?

Evie must have wondered about this, too. Over the roof of the car, we exchanged a look. She broke the silence. "The minister is a charming man. Watch him like a cobra, Maya."

CHAPTER 6

LARRY'S SEEDS

THE CLARK'S NUTCRACKER, a hard-working little bird, collects seeds from the whitebark pine in Yellowstone Park, thirty thousand pine nuts each year, and hides them for a winter day. It flies as far as fifteen miles away, drills the nuts into the ground in sets of ten, then places a stone on top of each stash to mark the spot. Ornithologists say the Clark's nutcracker remembers where it has secreted those thousands of morsels—70 percent of the time. Those it forgets about eventually start new whitebark pine forests. My father, Larry, has an even better memory than a Clark's nutcracker. He remembers just about everything, even long streams of numbers like bank accounts and GPS coordinates.

When I asked Larry to place the Down Dog Diary somewhere safe, I should have guessed that he would throw himself into the project as if he were diving into a pool of his favorite chocolate pudding. That was back in May, when Jorn and I had fought to protect the diary. I'd hurt people, and people dear to me had been hurt. That was when I decided it was best for the diary, and me, to live in separate places.

On the day we launched this plan, Larry and I met at his dining room table. In front of us were three books, one of them the diary. "Now, I've weighed and measured the diary and found two blank journals of similar size and heft," Larry explained. "I'll wrap each book in plain brown paper, mix them all up in a bag, and scatter them to the wind. I won't even know myself which one is which. Cool, huh?"

Evie, passing through on her way to her studio, drifted her fingertips across his shoulders and said, "Keep it simple, Larry."

"Yeah, yeah."

"Explain 'scatter to the wind,'" I said. "That sounds a bit haphazard."

"Three different hiding places. Three different cities." He tapped his head. "I'll keep that info right here."

"But what if something happens to you, like you're eaten by an alligator?" I asked.

"I've written down the locations and clues and hidden them somewhere in this house. You and Evie will find them."

This was beginning to sound like one of the games that had made the family software company, The Skyes the Limit, famous. It had all the markings of a quest. "So if I need the diary, and I'm probably desperate if I need it quickly, I first have to solve a puzzle to find it?"

"Neat, isn't it?" Larry beamed at me.

Hardly practical, I thought.

Now, it was two months later, and that desperate time had come. If I am to help Jorn find Gasquet, I will need all my weapons: my intuition, the answers I found in meditation, the skills I honed in tai chi and yoga, and the Down Dog Diary. I don't know how to explain it, but when I hold the diary in my hands, I feel more confident, more sure of the path to take.

So it was time to get the diary back.

We were lucky—Larry hadn't met up with a hungry gator in the wilds of Minnesota, so he could just hand me the clues, which he did at a family dinner. When Larry slid an envelope across the table toward me, my sensible sister said, "Good grief, Larry, do you have to be so dramatic? Just tell her where they are."

Larry was insulted. "That would take all the fun out of it."

Heart, who held no love for the diary and who, as the smart manager of the family business, had considerable experience reeling in crazy Larry ideas, said, "Fun? She should just dump that stupid diary on somebody else, and let them handle the problem. This family doesn't need it."

Eight-year-old Sadie sucked a string of spaghetti into her mouth. "You used the 's' word, Mama."

Heart looked baffled. Sadie whispered, "Stupid."

Heart turned from Sadie to David, her husband. He shrugged. "Well, you did."

Heart spent her days chasing "normal" and running as far as she could from the remnants of being raised in a community of peace-loving, free-spirited, home-schooled tree huggers. One of Heart's efforts to erase her Whispering Spirit Farm upbringing was a campaign to raise Sadie in a "well-adjusted home environment." Her guides in this project were the latest books and mama blogs on child development. Sadie rode the school bus (something Heart was still envious of), ate nutritious Heart-prepared sandwiches with happy faces drawn on the plastic bags, and was being trained that name-calling is never productive.

But sometimes the world *is* stupid, and sometimes you experience such loss that hatred becomes a part of you like a hardening in your arteries. You can try to dislodge it with pretty affirmations, meditation, therapy, but the only thing that softens and eventually melts away hatred is clarity, and that can't be forced or called up. That's just a waiting game. Some days, it's just easier to hug a tree.

Still, it was never wise to upset Heart's cart of dos and don'ts. Her life mission was to be the best mother of all time. So I winked at Sadie and stayed out of the discussion, but Heart was still shaking the bone of the diary like a determined dog.

"I mean it, Maya; don't drag that book back into our lives," she said. "Look what happened last time. Trouble, trouble, trouble."

I knew this was the scared young Heart speaking, the Heart who remembered how we kids told stories about the Down Dog Diary that James Tumblethorne kept locked in a trunk in his cabin at Whispering Spirit Farm. We were fascinated with it and feared it. It was obviously precious, being one of the few things in the commune secured by lock and key. While the other kids were caught up in the mystery of the Down Dog Diary, I was obsessed with what Tum wrote in this book of secrets. When I asked him one day about the contents, he said, "Just stuff. Messages to Spirit."

"You mean prayers?" I asked.

Tum looked embarrassed and hunched his bear-like shoulders. "And stuff about my life."

"Like an autobiography."

"Someday you'll read it and see," he promised. At that time, I had no idea that James Tumblethorne had chosen me to be his heir and the next keeper of the Down Dog Diary.

I know now that Tum had gained strength from the diary, just as I do.

I opened the envelope Larry had given me and pulled out a paper and a key.

Larry said, "Memorize that then eat it. The paper, not the key."

Sadie was intrigued by such dire instructions. She got out of her chair and leaned her skinny body against mine, snooping over my shoulder at the paper. "It's just a bunch of numbers and stuff about a waitress."

Heart and David craned to look. David immediately said, "The numbers are GPS coordinates." Of course, a simple street address would be too easy.

"C'mon," I said to Larry. "Save me some time. At least tell me what cities."

"Shortcuts will ruin your life, Maya," Larry said. I'd heard that one before. Never take the shortcut in one of Larry's games. You are just asking for trouble.

After a long look from Evie, he finally mumbled, "All right. Minneapolis, New York, and Paris."

"Paris? Really, Larry?" Evie shook her head. "If this were a real emergency, we wouldn't have time for transatlantic flights."

I cleared my throat. "Actually, I was headed to Paris anyway." They all turned to me, surprised. "I'm going with Jorn to talk to Gasquet's family."

Jorn had continued to send text messages to Gasquet, but they were all falling like stones into the cyber abyss. No reply. So it was time to take another approach.

Sadie edged closer. "Can I come to Paris with you?" she whispered. My niece loved all things French.

"Not this time, kid," I said.

Disappointed, she flopped back into her chair, propped her elbows on the table, and cupped her face. "*Je suis triste.*"

"I'll bring you a tiny Eiffel Tower."

"*Tres* cool," she said, brightening.

CHAPTER 7

THE BITE OF
THE DAFFODIL

I T WAS NOT EASY to stay exasperated with my game-loving father when he had that look of wonder on his face and jittered with excitement. Dressed in his favorite Queen-concert T-shirt, he stood at the first set of coordinates on the corner of Hennepin Avenue and Nicollet Mall, humming "Another One Bites the Dust." With the spryness of a man half his age, Larry dodged the Friday morning downtown traffic and strode into the Minneapolis Central Library. He said, with not a small touch of pride, "One of the largest per capita collections of any major city in the United States. I'd like to see somebody find the diary in here. More than two million items."

Built in 2006 with sustainability in mind—a concept that appealed to my ecologically minded parents—the library screamed Minnesota modern. It was boxy with a soaring contemporary canopy over the atrium, a "green" roof full of drought-resistant plants, and frosted glass panel windows depicting Minnesota prairie grasses, birch trees, and snowy branches. I, who so easily fell in love with the details of a Corinthian column or the curve of a Gothic arch, was not sure that I liked it.

The clue that went with these coordinates was: *The waitress said, "Today's special is four sides but no main course. Be with you in a flash, darlin'."* Knowing my father's love of planting obvious clues in his games when the gamer was likely to be looking for obscurity, I figured out that the diary wasn't in the "main course" of the library, and the "four sides" had to mean we should start our search on the fourth floor. It was no surprise when we found the diary on the fourth floor of the library in Special Collections, but I was taken aback to find it in the care of a librarian named Flash. I hadn't seen that one coming.

Flash, a gangly man who looked way too young to be a librarian, was wearing a short-sleeved plaid cotton shirt with a polka-dotted bow tie. He was one of Larry's groupies. Larry's online and gaming connections were vast. He was, after all, the creator of Peace Hero, Skyes the Limit's top-selling interactive game. After handing the wrapped diary to Larry, Flash launched into a stream of questions about gaming strategy that Larry would have eagerly indulged all day if I hadn't lured him away with the promise of lunch at his favorite Minneapolis burger joint.

Tucked into the back booth at the restaurant, I took out the diary and knew even before I unwrapped it that it was one of the fakes. No vibes. The Down Dog Dairy gives off an energy all its own; sometimes I even imagine a warmth when I handle it, like a living thing. This package had no life; it was one of the blank books. At my look of disappointment, Larry mumbled around a mouthful of onion ribbons, "One down, but isn't this fun?"

"Great father-daughter time," I replied, unwrapping the book anyway, lifting the cover of the blank journal, then breaking into a grin.

"What?" Larry leaned across the table, trying to see. I turned the journal toward him. On the first page was a drawing: a set of dentures with a single daffodil clutched in them. Larry snorted. "Evie. She always has to get in on my fun."

Something about the drawing made my intuition buzz. The longer I looked at it, the more I felt that it was important. I knew if I asked Evie what the drawing meant she would not give me an answer. She never explained her work, and besides, the connections Evie made on the easel were not always obvious even to Evie. Sometimes they simply surfaced—like a bubble of life-giving air or a dead fish.

I TOOK THE BLANK Daffodil Diary, as I now thought of it, along on my way to New York City and the next set of co-ordinates. On a Sunday flight scheduled to get us into the city by mid-afternoon, Jorn sat in the seat beside me zipping through a Saturday *New York Times* crossword he'd found in the waiting area at the gate in Minneapolis. When he finished, he stuffed it in the pocket of the seat in front of him and said, "You've been staring at that doodle since we got on the plane. What's bothering you?"

"Just wondering what Evie was trying to tell me."

"Does it have to mean anything? No offense, but your mother draws some weird stuff."

"True."

"But?"

"Evie doesn't intentionally do 'messages.'"

"So, you think her, what, subconscious is trying to tell you something?" Jorn really didn't like giving the subconscious that much credit. "What disturbs you about it? The teeth or the flower? Frankly, I think this is one of your mother's more benign drawings. I like the teeth. When I was a kid, I had a set of false teeth that you wound up, and they clacked all over the table." He demonstrated, forcing his mouth into a big grin and chomping at me.

I hadn't even thought about the set of dentures; it was the flower that caught my attention. "The daffodil is a symbol of new beginnings."

Jorn said, "And here we are, beginning a new adventure."

"It's also poisonous."

"That would take the clack out of you."

Many cultures considered daffodils lucky, I explained to Jorn, but only when presented in a bunch.

"So?"

I pointed to Evie's drawing. "A single daffodil portends misfortune."

CHAPTER 8

DINNER
WITH DARLING

W E WERE SCHEDULED TO be in New York for only a few hours; our flight to Paris left late that night. So we took a taxi straight to the second set of coordinates, a street corner in Queens. Standing on the sidewalk, the taxi long gone, our bags at our feet, Jorn leaned over my shoulder and read again the clue for this stop: *The grouchy waitress said, "Name's Paulette. I'd advise against the Eggs Benedict, unless you're feelin' adventurous."*

We scanned the block of brownstone apartments. Names were carved in the stone lintels above the entrances: Douglas Arms, Windsor Hall, Benedict Place. That had to be it. "There," I pointed to a well-maintained but old brick building.

"Let's give it a try," Jorn said. We hefted our bags and walked up the steps. There were six apartments in the three-story building; none of the names on the buzzers matched the name Paulette. Jorn started ringing doors. One intercom after another: "Is Paulette there? Is Paulette there?"

It was early evening, time when people wanted to be left alone with their remote and a beer, and our interruptions were not welcomed. With our ears still ringing from the caustic vocabulary of apartment four, we moved on to apartment five where our question elicited a pause and a gruff, "Who wants to know?" We had barely mentioned Larry's name when we were cut off by the buzzer unlocking the front door. There was no elevator, just steep, worn steps. On the top floor at apartment five, a spindly woman in a sea-foam green track suit, a burning cigarette clutched in her swollen-knuckled hands, leaned against the doorframe. Paulette.

Paulette's apartment seemed tiny mainly because books were crowding out the humans living there. Shelves, jammed with books, surged to the high ceiling. Books were piled in stacks around all the furniture and on every table. It was an excellent place to hide a diary. Sitting in the center of this nest of literature, on a Persian rug, was a cheetah.

"Don't mind Darlin'," said Paulette in an accent as thick as Texas toast. The big cat was still and watchful, not a muscle rippling, even when an emergency vehicle blasted down the narrow street outside. Paulette waved the cigarette in her hand, just missing her bleached blonde beehive. The smoke from her cigarette drifted toward the windows, which were flung open and barred with wrought iron, probably a good idea with Darling in the house. I'd never been this close to a cheetah and couldn't seem to take my eyes off the beautiful animal.

"She won't hurt you," reassured a large man obscuring the doorway to what must have been the kitchen. He motioned to his own chest. "Pavel. So you're friends with crazy Larry, huh?"

"He's my dad," I said. That brought life to Pavel, who crossed the room in three strides, pushed Jorn aside as if he were a paperclip, and wrapped me in a hug that lifted me off my feet. Jorn stepped forward to intervene without much success.

Pavel set me down gently, then settled me on the old sofa. "I got tea. You like tea?"

I nodded. He didn't ask Jorn what he wanted.

Paulette sank to the floor next to Darling and absently stroked the big cat, which kept its eyes on us. I didn't mind when Jorn sat down close beside me.

"So you're Evie's kid." Paulette shook her head in disbelief. She shot cigarette smoke out the side of her mouth, careful to keep it away from Darling's face. "You look like her."

As Pavel returned with a tray and cups of tea, Jorn asked, "How did you meet Evie?"

"We waitressed together. The Rusty Nail in LA, what a dump. Evie was sweet but clueless."

"Really," I replied, a note of offense in my voice.

"Straight from the farm, scared of her own shadow. She didn't know nothin' about the beauty process." I considered Paulette's expertise in this area: lilac eye shadow weighing down the lids of her faded blue eyes, foundation applied with a trowel, glaring red lipstick. Paulette was at least ten years older than Evie and looked twice that.

Paulette went on, "Taught her everything. Where to buy clothes, the cheap stuff that looked like a million bucks; how to put on her face; how to carry plates without burning the bejesus out of her arm. She broke more dishes that first month—" At the memory, Paulette's bright red lips slid into a grin. She stroked Darling, who had decided we were uninteresting and was cleaning her paw. Her loud purr vibrated through the room. "Evie was pretty once she got her face on. And she had that whole charisma thing going."

"Charisma?" I asked.

"She drew people to her. Had that natural way about her that made people relax, you know?"

I did know, but I had always thought that was a quality my mother had acquired while living at the commune. Evie was a spirit at peace; that was the kind of energy others sidled up to for warmth, healing, security. I knew Evie had lost her parents when she was young, and it suddenly dawned on me that I was looking at the mother of my mother, if not by birth then by love.

I finished my tea and set down my cup. Pavel offered more, but I shook my head. The cheetah's paw rested on Paulette's leg, its eyes drifting closed. Paulette relaxed into memories. "We had us some fun, Evie and me. I taught her how to sew, just like my mama taught me, and how to cook something fancier than those crappy ramen noodles. She tried to teach me how to draw; that was her thing. But I even make a mess of Hangman."

I gestured toward the books, probably thousands squeezed into the tiny apartment. "Evie likes to read. You seem to have that in common."

"Some of them are mine, but mostly they're Pavel's. He drives a taxi and always has a book with him."

Pavel shrugged with a small embarrassed smile. "Was teacher back in Russia."

Darling nudged Paulette's arm with her nose. Paulette started to get up, groaned, and suddenly Pavel was there lifting her to her feet. "Time to take Darlin' for a walk. Wanna come?"

I sure did. I'd never walked down a New York street, or any street, with a cheetah at my side.

"Be with you in a flash, Darlin'," she said, clipping a leash to the big cat's rhinestone collar. Darling rose in anticipation and padded to the door, leash dragging on the floor. I noticed that she limped. The cheetah is the fastest land animal in the world; it's built for speed—long legs eating up the earth at seventy miles per hour, slender body streaking past, a blur of beauty. It depended on its bursts of speed to hunt its prey—to survive. With a limp like that, Darling wouldn't last long in the wild.

As Paulette stepped into another room, Pavel saw me eyeing Darling with a frown. "Damn circus," he said. "Darling's previous owner bad man. Not fix her broken leg right. Now she old and full of arthritis. She a Paulette project."

From the other room, Paulette shouted, "If people didn't screw up so much, I wouldn't have to keep fixin' their shit."

Pavel gave us a grin and rubbed his cue ball smooth head. It seemed my young mother had also been a Paulette project.

I bet Pavel was one, too. Or, judging by the way his eyes softened when they lit on Paulette and the way his big hands lifted her to her feet and waited for her old knees to remember how to work, maybe Paulette was a Pavel project.

A few minutes later, Paulette returned, having donned a fresh layer of makeup. "All set." She had traded her track suit for pressed jeans and a simple black T-shirt. I looked at her feet and swallowed a laugh. She wore penny loafers, just like the ones Evie always wore.

During our walk, Darling alternately terrified and amazed a good four blocks of jaded New Yorkers. Paulette ignored the looks. "Is it legal to keep a cheetah as a pet?" I asked.

"Not anymore, at least in the US," Paulette said. "But I consider Darlin' grandfathered in, and nobody's come knockin' on my door yet. So I say live and let live. Me and Darlin' are just keepin' company, two old broads with bum legs."

Upon hearing her name, Darling looked up at us with her beautiful brown eyes and bumped Paulette's hip with her head.

When we returned to the apartment, Pavel had dinner ready and Jorn had set the table. After the stroganoff was gone and the hearty bread was reduced to crumbs, Pavel rose and walked over to a set of five thick leather-bound books on one of the book shelves. He plucked the middle one from the group, brought it back to the table, and handed it to me.

Settling back into his chair and lifting his wineglass to his lips, he watched me with anticipation. "Open."

Paulette indicated the book with her beer bottle. "Larry said you might be coming for this, but we didn't think so soon."

The title of the book was *The Mysterious Lives of Insects: From Ancient Times to Today*. Today appeared to be around 1890. When I opened the book, I found a cavity carved out of the pages and hiding in the hollowed-out book was a brown-wrapped package, just like the one Flash had given Larry and me at the Minneapolis Central Library.

"You tell Larry I cut up favorite book to keep his secret," Pavel said. "Made me greatly sad."

Seeing a small grin play across his kind face, I said, "I'm sure he'd want to buy you another one."

Pavel pushed the thought aside. "Not necessary. Can never repay Evie and Larry."

I tilted my head in question.

"They got us out of LA," Paulette said. "Pavel hated that town."

Pavel shook his head. "No history there. No old buildings. Just highways."

"New York suits Pavel better. The grouchy people, the rain and snow, the smell."

Pavel agreed. "Like grouchy and smells. California too bright."

"And, frankly, I was getting too old to wait tables. Didn't have the legs for it anymore. So, when Pavel and me had enough of LA, Evie and Larry bought us this place," said Paulette, glancing around her as if she still couldn't believe that she lived in such a home. "I never owned my own house. Always lived in dumpy apartments, even when I was a kid." Paulette took a swig of beer. "Never thought I'd be livin' in a palace like this."

I lifted the package from its hiding place. The energy

poured through the folds of the brown wrapping, making my hands tingle. I smiled at Jorn, who instantly knew something had happened.

It was the Down Dog Diary.

CHAPTER 9

CELEBRATE
THE ORDINARY

I N ANCIENT EGYPT, PET cheetahs were trained as hunters. In shamanic terms, the cheetah spirit reminds us to move, respond quickly, and stay focused. Unsure whether it was because I had just crossed paths with a cheetah or because I had the diary in my hands again, I was nevertheless alert. Sleep eluded me on the eight-hour flight from New York's JFK to Charles De Gaulle Airport in Paris. Jorn, on the other hand, did not have the same problem. I elbowed him again to put an end to his symphony of snores and snorts.

In the dark cabin, while those all around me slept, I slipped the diary from my satchel and clicked on the overhead lamp. The diary, which was only slightly larger than my hand, appeared fragile; however, I knew it was anything but. The black cover and yellowed pages were soft with use and age. When space was limited, those before me had written between the lines and inching up the sides of the pages. I untied the leather cord holding the pages together and opened the Down Dog Diary.

Chanting mentally and paging through the diary eventually brought me a sense of peace, high in the sky. The words drifted in and out of my mind, and the smells wrapped my head like a turban. I stopped to read one page and the scent of a summer bonfire, like the ones we often had growing up, twisted into my senses. Back then, I loved to poke the fire with a long stick, releasing sparks of burning light into the night dark. My sister, Heart, never played with fire. She stayed back. Every once in a while, she'd warn, "Watch out, Maya," but I would ignore her, preferring to live on the edge of light than sit with my sister in the dark.

I turned my head toward Jorn and found his eyes open, watching me in the dim light of the cabin. "You think you're going to find some magic in there?" he asked softly. "Something to help us find Gasquet?"

The scents of the diary eluded Jorn. He felt nothing special when holding it, and the words did not reach inside him and find a place of rightness. He thought it was nonsense, but he knew the nonsense was important to me so when I had insisted we go on this scavenger hunt, he had given me one of his long-suffering looks but hadn't objected. Despite his acquiescence to my intuition, the diary tested the balance of Jorn's logic, which he relied on in work and in tracking dead friends.

I had become familiar with some of the authors in the book, but I did not recognize the handwriting on the page delivering the memory of smoke. The entry, dated in the 1960s, said, "And the beat goes on. Slow and incessant. It's a native drum, a pesky drip, a mother's love." I read the passage to Jorn.

Jorn shook his head. "Reading that thing is like diving into a barrel of fortune cookies."

"Evie says you can find wisdom anywhere, even in the produce section of the grocery store. The trick is to be open to it."

Then I told him about Ida, a woman at Whispering Spirit who read the Bible every day. "She opened the Good Book to a random page and then prayed on what she read. She said it was God talking to her."

"God guided her to the day's message," Jorn said.

"You don't sound surprised."

"I've seen 'God' guide a lot of people into weird shit," he said.

Passengers were waking from the night's uncomfortable rest, making their way to one of the plane's tiny rest rooms to freshen up, and the flight attendants had begun rolling out breakfast: croissants, juice, coffee. I slid the diary back into my satchel.

Jorn rubbed the sleep from his eyes. "I don't know why Madame Dubois insisted we meet at the Louvre. Seems rather public."

"What are you going to say to her?"

"I don't know. Sorry I didn't take better care of your son?" He flipped down the tray in front of him and smiled his thanks to the attendant, who handed him a cup of coffee.

"Stop it. You did the best you could. You were wounded and unconscious."

"So, I was the lucky one, and her son was not. No mother wants to hear that."

"We still don't know if this is Gasquet playing a game with us or someone who has stolen his identity. The important thing is to find out what the person who sent you that message wants and how we can help him."

Jorn peered out the airplane's tiny window looking down on a carpet of clouds. "Maybe Gasquet's mother has heard from him. If I can just talk to him . . ."

WE RODE THE METRO, packed with Monday morning commuters, from the airport to the Rive Gauche or Left Bank. We had three hours before we were due to meet Madame Dubois, just enough time to find a guest house, shower off the long, sticky flight, and grab a buttery, fresh-baked croissant at a nearby *patisserie*.

We took a taxi to the Louvre, squeezing our eyes shut at the near misses that either inflamed or amused our driver. As Jorn paid the fare, I looked up at the Louvre's glass pyramid and the ornate palace that embraced it and sighed. It was always like this. I couldn't wait to get inside.

Being surrounded by greatness was a meditation, Evie always said, and she was right. Stepping through the doors of the Louvre, I felt the usual art-induced calm settle on me. Avoiding Mona and Venus, the usual suspects drawing the crowds, we consulted a map of the museum and made our way through miles of masterpieces to the Galerie

Médicis. This was the place Madame Marie-Jacques Dubois, mother of Gasquet, had chosen for our rendezvous.

Between 1622 and 1625, Flemish artist Peter Paul Rubens painted more than twenty-four canvases depicting the life of Marie de Médici, the Italian-born queen of France. Marie, who commissioned this work, made sure she came off well: regal, magnificent, and linked to divinity. Today the long, quiet room was empty except for an art student intently copying one of the paintings in his sketchpad and an older woman perched on a padded bench. Dwarfed by the huge paintings of struggle and triumph, she waited, back straight, smart leather handbag secure on her lap.

"Madame Dubois?" Jorn asked, approaching the woman with an outstretched hand and a gentle smile.

Remaining seated, the woman considered him for a moment then, with a slight tip of her head, placed her hand in his. It was a gracious gesture. An audience was granted. Jorn introduced himself, then me, and we settled on the bench beside her. Gasquet's mother looked at home among the regal and dramatic images. Beautiful, proud, with the easy elegance of a Frenchwoman, she wore a Carolina Herrera floral damask dress and an ornate pearl and diamond-studded gold cross that looked as if it had been ripped from the neck of Marie de Médici herself.

"Gasquet loves coming here," she said in accented English. "Ever since he was a boy I bring him." She motioned to the nearby student. "My Gasquet likes to draw and study. When I miss him too much, I come here."

Jorn nodded. "Gasquet's always dragging me to museums, no matter where we are. He can talk about art for hours."

I noticed that, like Madame Dubois, Jorn had slipped into present tense when speaking of Gasquet.

A smile tugged at the woman's lips then faded. A hand drifted up to cover the cross at her neck. "Tell me. Where is my son? He has not called in many months, and I am worried. I thought he would be with you."

Jorn hesitated. Madame Dubois's expression was puzzled, expectant, hopeful. Her neat appearance, her straight posture, the way she waited for an explanation indicated a fondness for organization, a healthy personal esteem, and a sense of entitlement. Although her frame and aura were fragile, I felt a strength in Madame Dubois, an energy tethered by fine control. I was sure that she had not told her husband she was meeting us today.

As Jorn was about to answer her, a man strode up, and for a moment, Jorn and I were too stunned to speak. Jorn slowly rose from the bench. It was Gasquet.

Madame Dubois turned and held out a welcoming hand toward the man.

"This is my son René," said Madame Dubois. "Gasquet's younger brother."

René leaned down and kissed his mother on both cheeks. Then with an open smile, he pumped Jorn's hand and nodded toward me. "Sorry, sorry. I'm late."

Jorn stuttered for a moment. "I-I-I'm sorry, but you look so much like him."

René grinned and shrugged. "That's what they say." He brushed a hand through his short, salon-styled hair. "Except Gasquet refuses to cut those dreads of his. Likes looking the rebel."

I thought back to the photo of Gasquet. Jorn had explained that Gasquet's mother was French, and his father was Cameroonian. Both sons favored their father. I saw the resemblance between René and Gasquet—the same bronze skin, the same nose, the same build—but the brother was tensely wired where Gasquet was loose-limbed, René was more serious where Gasquet carried a joke on the tip of his tongue. But the biggest difference was in the eyes. René lacked Gasquet's inviting brown eyes. There was nothing irrepressible in René Dubois's eyes.

As Jorn sat and tried to regain his equilibrium, I asked, "Are you a photographer, too, René?"

"I am an art dealer, a businessman who is lucky enough to spend his days surrounded by beauty," he smiled again and gestured toward the art around him.

Madame Dubois pulled René's arm until he sat down beside her. "He owns a very successful *galerie*."

"It better be successful or *Papa* would have my head," René laughed, but I noticed Madame Dubois tensed at his words. He glanced around the gallery. "So where's Gasquet? He has been quite the mystery man lately."

Jorn and I exchanged looks. Taking a breath, Jorn began, "The last time I saw Gasquet was more than nine months ago in the Hindu Kush mountains of Afghanistan. We were ambushed on the way to an interview. Both of us were wounded."

Madame Dubois gasped and reached for René; the hand on the cross tightened.

Jorn continued, "We got separated. I lost consciousness, was found, and turned over to American troops. I woke up in a hospital in Germany. I haven't seen, or heard, from Gasquet since."

My breath hitched at Jorn's lie, but I kept my face still.

"Nine months ago?" whispered Madame Dubois. She turned to her son. "René, where is your brother?"

René asked Jorn, "Wounded, you say? You do not know if he is dead or alive?" At the word "dead," Madame Dubois stiffened.

Jorn shook his head. "I'm sorry. I had hoped he had been in contact with you."

"*Non*," René said. "We have heard nothing. Have you talked to his editors?"

"I've called all his usual contacts at the magazines and newspapers, but—nothing."

René frowned. "You would think they would at least notify *us* that Gasquet was missing."

"One editor said he contacted you looking for Gasquet."

René glanced at his mother then shook his head. "*Non.* He is mistaken. This is the first we have heard of this."

Madame Dubois had begun worrying the cross at her throat. She turned pleading eyes on her son. "René, you must look for your brother. I don't know what I would do if . . . he could be anywhere, hurt, my dear Gasquet." René wrapped his arm around his mother and pulled her close.

"I will take care of this, *Maman*," René reassured her.

Jorn explained the avenues he'd already explored to no avail—the reporters and editors both he and Gasquet knew, his military contacts, his civilian sources in Afghanistan. "I thought you might know of a friend or a family member he would turn to."

"Gasquet can be . . . difficult," René said, with a frown. "As stubborn as our father. We have not seen or spoken to Gasquet in more than a year."

"May I ask why?" I asked.

"It has been terrible," said Madame Dubois, turning her attention to me, one woman seeking the support of another. "Gasquet and Aristide, his father, have never seen eye to eye. Their last argument was vicious. The words that were spoken." She lifted her fingers to her lips as if she could capture the words and take them back.

"According to my father, he is never wrong," René said. "He wanted Gasquet to come back to Paris, give up all this 'jet setting,' and head the photography department at my father's advertising agency. When Gasquet said no, *Papa* offered to set him up in his own studio. Perhaps taking wedding photos."

Jorn looked shocked and no wonder. A man who found nourishment in the paintings of the Louvre would have starved in a life of posing happy couples.

"Gasquet would have none of it. Stormed out of the house. And he didn't leave empty handed."

"*Non*, René, do not bring this up," Madame Dubois warned.

"Why not? It's a valuable family heirloom."

"What was it?" Jorn asked.

"A small sculpture. French. From the tomb of a powerful duke."

Jorn shook his head. "I never saw anything like that in Gasquet's possession."

René looked at Jorn intently. I thought he was about to

claim that he didn't believe Jorn, but then he relaxed and said, "Well, it disappeared the night my brother left." René lifted a shoulder. "I do not know if Gasquet took it or not. Our father refuses to talk about it."

I turned to Madame Dubois. "Is this why we are meeting here? You don't want Monsieur Dubois to know?"

Madame Dubois nodded then reached out to me, grasping my hand in a surprisingly strong grip. "That and because this place is a favorite haunt for Gasquet and me. My husband refuses to even talk about Gasquet. I do not understand it. Pride hardens the heart. But I am like water, dripping, dripping on my husband's resistance. Aristide will make up with Gasquet someday."

"I believe he will," I said, giving her hand a squeeze.

A sad sigh escaped her lips. "I miss my son. He sends me postcards from faraway places with silly song lyrics on the back. I read the cards over and over. The songs become stuck in my head."

"Beatles?" Jorn asked.

"*Oui*, and others. Ones I sang to him in the nursery."

"When was the last time you received a postcard from Gasquet?" I asked.

"Too long ago." Madame Dubois searched the paintings all around us, as if seeking strength. Her eyes met Jorn's. "You will find my son? Tell him to send me more cards?"

Jorn nodded. "Of course."

Something in Jorn's assurance soothed Madame Dubois. We all rose from the museum bench. Madame Dubois reached up and kissed Jorn on both cheeks, then did the same to me. "I pray you will find him, Peter. Godspeed to both of you."

The Duboises left with promises to stay in touch. René asked to trade business cards; I had none so I wrote my email and phone number on the back of Jorn's card. René had a business trip to America planned and said he would drop in to see us if he had time.

Still standing in the Galerie Médicis, I looked up at the huge paintings: so thoroughly Baroque, so sensual, so complex and pulsing with aspiration.

"Did Gasquet like this style of painting?" I asked Jorn.

"What?" Jorn, staring at the backs of René and Madame Dubois as they left the gallery, brought his focus back to the hall of paintings. "No, not at all."

"What then? Show me what Gasquet would have come here to see."

We consulted a directory and then Jorn led me to the second floor of the Louvre, the Sully Wing. "Chardin," Jorn said, pointing to a painting before us. "He loved Jean-Baptiste Chardin."

I admitted I didn't know much about the French painter.

"Chardin was Gasquet's hero. Gasquet loved the idea of seeing beauty in the everyday," Jorn explained. "A master of the still life, Chardin wasn't afraid to rock the eighteenth-century French art world. No Rococo painting for him. Forget the king, Chardin said, give me kitchen maids and children and a bloody fish dangling from a hook on the wall."

"Chardin revered the ordinary."

"Yeah," Jorn said. "Just like Gasquet. Slice of life; quiet, revealing moments."

As we were leaving the Louvre, walking past the modern

steel and glass pyramid in the Cour Napoléon, I said to Jorn, "You didn't tell Gasquet's mother and brother about the text message. Why not?"

Jorn paused before answering. "I don't know."

CHAPTER 10

RINGO SENT ME

JORN WAS PENSIVE DURING dinner that evening, absently tearing off chunks of crusty baguette and slipping them to the stray dog beneath our sidewalk table. While he fed the wildlife, I studied the nightlife—people passing on the narrow sidewalk inches from our dinner of wine-poached salmon with black truffles and chicken francaise. The energy of Paris—busy and preoccupied like most big cities—was threaded with a sense of golden delight in just being alive. Companions leaned a little closer, whispered a little more. Shopkeepers shrugged at patrons and pretended indifference. Old women swayed and flirted with young men tied to their earbuds. This *joie de vivre* is yoga in action: it is realizing that this moment that we are in is—wondrous.

Jorn, however, paid no attention to the soft evening

breeze, the glow of the streetlamps, the lively music drifting to us from a restaurant down the street. Lost in thought, he poked at his salmon and asked, "What did you think of the Duboises?"

"Obviously, Marie-Jacques Dubois is a woman in pain. She is beautiful, refined, and strong," I said. "She loves her sons, would protect them at all costs, and probably has sided with them a time or two against her husband. Gasquet, though, is her favorite."

That stopped Jorn, his hand paused in the act of sneaking another chunk of bread to the flea-infested hound. The dog whined and watched the tidbit frozen in time. "Why do you say that?"

"It's in her voice when she says Gasquet's name. She loves René, too, but he is not the firstborn, the first to steal her heart."

"And René?"

"Practical man, caring son, indifferent brother."

"He did seem more concerned about a family heirloom than finding his brother." Jorn dropped the bread, which the dog snatched from the air.

Slicing a piece of perfectly prepared chicken that was definitely not destined for the beggar under the table, I said, "René suspects you know more than you're telling them."

"Gasquet usually changed the subject when it came to family, but I got the impression they were rich and opinionated. He said everyone was a strategist in the Dubois family."

"Except for Gasquet?"

Jorn thought about it for a moment. "Gasquet was *joie de vivre*, squared."

"It doesn't sound like the Gasquet in the text message," I said.

"That's what's worrying me. What's happened to him? Did he send that message or did someone else? If he's not trying to contact me, who is? And why?"

I WOKE, SQUEEZED IN my morning yoga practice in the small space beside my bed, and dressed. Then I stepped out of the quiet of our charming guest house into the fresh morning air and strolled down the crooked cobblestone alley to the Boulevard Saint-Michel. I could smell the Seine and headed toward it, nodding good morning to a sidewalk artist either starting his day or closing down his night. Chalk in hand, he was drawing Jesus in a red evening gown with a feather in his hair.

For a long time, I stood at the river's edge and stared across the water at the Cathedral of Notre Dame, enchanted, as usual, by its massive beauty. It was my favorite church in the world. I always stopped at Notre Dame whenever I was in Paris, to sit for a moment, to absorb the warm light flowing through the stained glass, to draw in the restful energy. Even the whisperings of Notre Dame's ever-present tourists and the clicking of their incessant picture taking could not break its spell.

After spending a good half-hour in the contentment of Notre Dame, I left with a nod to a gargoyle or two and walked back to the guest house. Shopkeepers were sweeping sidewalks in front of their stores. Delivery trucks rattled down narrow roads. The woman at the *patisserie* was full of smiles as she sold me breakfast croissants and coffee to help Jorn start the day.

Our flight left for the States that night. Before then, we had two missions: visit Gasquet's apartment and check out the last set of coordinates provided by Larry.

"Why are we doing this again?" Jorn asked, looking up at the discrete front of a French bank, the final location in Larry's scavenger hunt. "You already have the diary."

"I want to see what Evie drew in the third journal."

Over a lunch of sharp cheese, perfect wine, and amazing bread bought at a *boulangerie* and eaten in a little park full of children and chess players, we studied Larry's final clue: *The waitress said, "That Too Loose fellow won't pay his bill. You can bank on it. Stiffed me for 54,200 francs just last night."*

The "Too Loose fellow" was a reference to French painter Henri Toulouse-Lautrec. The coordinates led us to a small financial institution, Banque Harden-Lautrec. The key Larry had given me opened safety deposit box number 54200, home of the third book. On the first page of the blank journal was another drawing: two crows, facing each other, mirror images of mystery.

AFTER VISITING THE BANK, we rode the Metro to Montmartre. Then, on foot, we navigated twisting alleys and narrow rues to Gasquet's apartment, an old building with cracked stonework and petite balconies not even big enough for a single chair.

"Do you have a plan to get in?" I asked.

"Don't get out your lock pick set yet," Jorn said. "Let's try something legal first." I'd learned the finer points of illegal entry from a boy in the Whispering Spirit commune, and I had discovered recently that if you are the keeper of the Down Dog Diary, it was a handy skill to have.

Jorn knocked on the door. After several moments, punctuated by banging noises and muttering, a woman with a coppery dye job opened the door. Short and shaped like a tub, she filled the space of the doorway, waiting. Jorn greeted her in French. She did not reply, just eyed us, her lips clamped on a drooping cigarette.

Jorn explained that he was a friend of Gasquet's and had been told that if he ever needed to use the apartment, he could. The landlady was not buying it. Jorn had been here before but always with Gasquet, and during those visits, he'd not met the landlady. I took out my smartphone and showed her the photo of Jorn and Gasquet. "*Mes amis*," I said, pointing to the photo. Friends.

The woman responded with a stream of French, which basically wondered if we thought she was an idiot, a fool who did not know about Photoshop and other American tricks. She said she maintained respectable apartments and didn't let just anyone in, especially not Americans with their phony photographs on their phones. Jorn held up his hands, making peace and smiling. "But I know the password," he said in French.

This stopped the woman's tirade. "*Mot de passe?*" she asked, removing the cigarette from her lips for the first time. Her look dared Jorn to come up with the watchword.

He smiled. "Ringo. Ringo sent me."

Upon hearing those magical words, suspicion drained

from the woman's eyes and they filled with bonhomie. Suddenly, she was waving us in, not only into the building but into her apartment, a dark, crowded affair smothered in too much furniture, too many fringed lampshades, and the odor of garlic. She went to a lady's desk, pulled down the hinged front, and reached into one of the cubbyholes. With a flourish, she presented Jorn with an ornate key then offered us biscuits and coffee. We declined. "*Merci, merci, mais non.*"

As we climbed the stairs to Gasquet's apartment, I looked back and found Gasquet's landlady watching us from her doorway. She waved her cigarette at me.

Gasquet's apartment was on the second floor facing the street. He was considered a good tenant. He'd rented the same apartment for years now, always paying for the full year in advance. Jorn said Gasquet worried about being out of the country on assignment when the rent came due. "He was obsessive about keeping his bills paid up," Jorn said.

"Or he didn't want to run afoul of the landlady," I said. "She's a hard case."

Jorn fiddled with the stubborn lock and, finally, opened the door. He entered first with a shout, "Hello, anybody home?"

Silence and a musty scent greeted us.

The layout was similar to the landlady's apartment, but where hers was dark, Gasquet's was light; where she crammed in more than she needed, Gasquet settled for the bare necessities; and where hers reeked of garlic, his smelled of disuse. Gasquet's décor was modern, black leather sofa and chairs, rugs in bright geometric patterns. The walls were painted white, a canvas for a gallery of photos, Gasquet's I presumed, all in plain black frames with white mats. Nothing to distract from the images. Jorn moved deeper into the apartment, stopping at one photo after another. He probably had been there when Gasquet took most of these images. Maybe he had been the one to make those village children laugh as Gasquet clicked away or the one to talk them past that checkpoint with the stern-looking soldier, a dab of that day's lunch still on his lip.

"He's really good, isn't he?" I said.

"He has that gift—capturing our secrets in a look." Jorn shook his head in admiration at the image of Iraqi children playing soccer with American soldiers. Everyone was grinning, except for one small girl, in sharp focus in the foreground. Wrapped in a long dress and headscarf, she watched the game with longing.

"You remember many of these," I said.

"Yeah." He straightened one of the frames. "This one. The Taliban destroyed a giant Buddha carved into a hillside. Two thousand years old. Shot to pieces. Gasquet and I couldn't believe it. G snapped pictures, tears streaming down his face, until a Taliban officer ordered us to stop."

I remembered the story. Perhaps I had even read Jorn's account of the incident. And I remembered Evie's sadness at such a loss, not just to Buddhists but to the world. "When will people get it?" she had said. "Cultural destruction equals human destruction."

"To Gasquet, killing art was almost as bad as killing people." Jorn lifted his shoulders. "He said at least people could fight back."

Jorn turned away from the photograph and looked around the empty apartment. "Where is he?"

"You expected him to be here."

"Or at least some sign of him." Jorn swept his hand over a dusty table. "But he hasn't been here in a while."

I walked around the apartment, stopping to look at a spot on the hardwood floor, then crouched for a closer look. It didn't fit in this obsessively neat home. "Look at this." I pointed to the floor. Jorn squatted next to me. It was blood, just a few drops, but surely the tidy Gasquet would not have left this and gone off on assignment. Someone had cut himself. Jorn and I searched for more bloody evidence. There was nothing in Gasquet's laundry basket. I opened the cabinet below the kitchen sink and found a trash bin. Inside was a single paper towel with more dried blood.

I was puzzled. There was not enough blood to indicate a serious wound, and there was no indication of a struggle.

Jorn scanned the walls and straightened another frame, this one a photo of a scrawny cat eyeing the wares of a fish stall. He approached a desk in the corner and began going through it. He found a razor blade with blood on it. "I think someone was searching through the desk and cut himself with this blade. I nearly did the same thing. There's another spot of blood on the lip of the drawer."

"So the apartment has been searched."

Jorn nodded. "Someone's been here looking for something. Perhaps a wall safe. Some of the picture frames are askew. G would never have tolerated that." Jorn ran his fingers along the edges of Gasquet's CD collection. "They're out of order. G always alphabetized his music; I used to tease him about it. Yes, someone's been here."

I turned and examined the image next to me—a foggy night in Montmarte. I gave it a tap to straighten it. "Whoever they are, they don't seem to be too concerned about getting caught," I said. "I mean they just pitched the paper towel in the trash. Wouldn't a professional take it with him to avoid leaving his DNA behind?"

"I don't know the protocol for burglars, and I don't watch many crime dramas."

We took another spin through the small one-bedroom apartment: neatly made bed, no food in the refrigerator, no plants, no dirty clothes lying around, the trash empty except for the bloody paper towel. No sign of Gasquet in residence. The apartment felt closed up, just as someone would do before taking a long trip.

Seeing a pile of envelopes, opened and dated months ago, on the desk, I asked Jorn, "Where's his recent mail?"

We searched the apartment and came up with nothing. Finally, we locked the door behind us and returned the key to the landlady. We asked her about any visitors, but she said no one but us.

"Do you collect Gasquet's mail?" asked Jorn.

"*Oui*," she said. "I have a key to his box. Every few months his brother comes by and picks it up to send on. Gasquet travels a lot, you know."

"Does René also visit the apartment?" I asked.

The woman shrugged. "Who knows? Is possible. I go dancing at night."

We left the apartment house and started our winding way back to the Metro station. Jorn had his head down in thought.

"I'm sorry he wasn't there," I said.

He simply shrugged.

Jorn's phone pinged. A text message. Jorn read it and stopped.

"What is it?"

He turned his phone for me to read the message: *Why did you leave me?*

CHAPTER 11

THE INVASION

ANY YEARS AGO, MY parents founded Whispering Spirit Farm in New Mexico, a community dedicated to the hippie values of live and let live, the Zen principles of planetary responsibility, and an incredibly naive do-it-yourself attitude. My mother, having been raised on a farm, knew a few things about growing food, but my father had never held a hammer in his life. Despite all odds, Larry developed into a fair handyman.

Today he was using those construction skills to install my shiny new secret safe. I had decided to keep the diary with me. Just because someone had come after it before didn't mean every loony was destined to show up on my doorstep, I told Larry. At the moment, my desire to keep the diary close outweighed my need to take elaborate measures (such as global scavenger hunts) to keep it secure. I decided to trust in Spirit to help me be a good keeper of the Down Dog Diary.

Larry had cut a hole in the wall of my living room for the most secure and fire resistant safe he could buy. With an electronic keypad lock as well as a biometric fingerprint reading lock, it was considerably more high tech than my previous hiding place for the one-hundred-year-old Down Dog Diary—wrapped in a pretty scarf and stashed behind some loose bricks in the wall of the yoga studio.

Although the safe was impressive, my hammer-wielding father in safety goggles and tool belt delighted more in building the swinging bookcase to disguise it. "This is so cool," he grinned, through a layer of dust and wood shavings. He swung the bookcase open and closed, open and closed, with not a whisper of sound. "I want one of these."

"What would you put in a safe?" I asked, watching as Bella the cat gleefully rolled in the sawdust, pausing only for the occasional body-shaking sneeze.

"Beats me."

Larry was extremely security conscious when it came to his wife and daughters, but as for material goods—a gang could back up a van to his house and clean him out (even his beloved computers) and he would meet the news with indifference. Things can be replace, he would say, not people. I don't know if this mellow attitude was because my father had never known poverty—he'd been born rich and gifted with the talent to make himself even richer—or if it was simply a hippie thing, giving the one-finger salute to the material world.

I heard the studio door open downstairs and assumed it was Jorn. I hadn't heard from him since we got back from Paris. Maybe he had news. But the authoritative voice that bellowed up the stairs was not Jorn's.

"Lawrence Harrison Skye the Third?"

Larry jerked, the head of the hammer missing the nail and finding his thumb. He smothered a curse and whipped the thumb into his mouth. Guilt flashed across his features, and he actually looked as if he wanted to hide.

"Who—?"

Larry leaped toward me and slapped a finger against my lips. "Shhh. Not a word. Maybe she'll go away."

"Lawrence, I know you're here," said the voice.

Larry's shoulders sank. "Dang that Evie," he whispered. "She ratted us out."

"Larry, who is that?" I lowered my voice to match his.

Larry gave me a half-guilty look. "That," he said, "is your grandmother."

Stunned, I said, "I have a grandmother?"

Larry paused as if he wanted to say more, but from the stairs came, in an even more insistent voice than before, "Lawrence?"

He turned way and started down the apartment's spiral staircase to the studio below, each dragging step weighted, a man headed to the guillotine. Bella and I hurried after him.

When he reached the bottom step, he nodded, "Mother."

The woman standing in the middle of the foyer of Breathe did not seem to mind that her son had not rushed to greet her with open arms. The word that came to mind when I first laid eyes on my grandmother was—imperious. Shaped like an expensive gift box in a lavender Chanel summer suit with classic pearl buttons, she regarded us with chin tilted. A matching pillbox hat was nested in her silver curls and, like the Queen Mother, a white leather handbag dangled from her arm.

"Mother, what are you doing here?" Larry asked.

Her chin lifted another regal quarter inch. "I came to collect you for dinner, Lawrence. Evangeline dropped me off. You are expected as well, Maya." My brows rose. She knew my name.

"I mean," Larry said, "in Gabriel's Garden."

"We can discuss that at dinner," she said, eyeing the hammer in Larry's dusty hand, the goggles pushed up on his forehead, and the torn, stretched-out T-shirt he'd thrown on for this dirty job. "Get cleaned up, Lawrence, and we'll go."

Without a word and shoulders drooping, Larry obediently turned and started upstairs to the apartment. I was shocked. What was going on here? I'd never seen Larry cowed. Who was this woman who could leach the beautiful spirit from my father with her presence? I automatically kicked in to protective mode, arming myself with deep breaths, ready to combat this relative from hell.

While Larry made himself presentable, my grandmother explored my domain. I followed her. She stopped in front of a painting of a woman sitting in a floating lotus flower or, if considered from a darker perspective, a lotus that appeared to be devouring a woman. "Is Evie still painting these disturbing pictures?" she asked with disdain.

"I wouldn't call it disturbing. Evie's art has—" I paused, "personality."

Perhaps not accustomed to someone disagreeing with her, my grandmother turned and studied me as if I were nestled in a giant lotus. She gave me a patronizing half-smile. "How kind."

Continuing her inspection of my business and home, she walked slowly around the desk where students checked in and got their passes stamped. She poked her head inside one of the cubbies for coats and shoes. She circled the studio slowly, stopping for several moments in front of the table with the Buddha and candles, but said nothing. Finally, she returned to the place where she had started and nodded toward the spiral staircase. "You live up there, I suppose."

Bella rubbed against my leg. I picked her up and said, "Yes."

"With that creature?" Apparently, like my sister, Grandmother was not a pet person.

Since I'd saved Bella the kitten from a watery grave on a cold March afternoon, she had grown into her name. Part Siamese and part curiosity, she had stunning blue eyes, soft champagne fur with brown-tipped ears and tail, and a nose that got into everything. She never did anything by halves, never withheld her love when she was mad and never met a bowl of food that couldn't be dispatched in one inhalation.

"Her name is Bella," I said, then added, "you can pet her if you like."

Grandmother gave me an incredulous look and, once again, examined my home.

"You don't think living in an old fire station isn't a bit—odd."

I shook my head.

My grandmother announced, "I prefer Victorian-style architecture myself."

Then with another withering glance at my home, she offered, "Perhaps I could buy you something more—comfortable. For your birthday."

My birthday was in June, a month ago. I had turned thirty-six. Evie, Heart, and Sadie had baked my favorite chocolate cake. David and Larry had come through with their traditional gift: pots of geraniums, petunias, and verbena for the patio behind the fire station. And Jorn had given me a novel about a consulting wizard, an unusual gift for a reporter who didn't believe in magic.

"Thank you, Grandmother, but Bella and I like it here."

She leaned toward me and lowered her voice. "It could be our little secret."

I saw something in her eyes, the lollipop in a stranger's hand, and laughed. Who knew I had an evil grandmother?

EVIE WAS AN OCCASIONAL wine drinker, but this evening she had passed "occasional" two glasses ago. Neither Heart nor I trusted her with knives so we volunteered to finish the salad.

"Are you sure?" she asked, her eyes begging us not to send her to her doom in the living room where Larry was entertaining Grandmother.

"Positive," we said. With a look that made both Heart and me feel guilty, she left the kitchen.

After she was gone, I leaned against the granite counter and asked my sister, "Why haven't I ever met Gran?"

Heart didn't look up as she tore the lettuce, piece by careful piece. "Grandmother. Not Grandma. And never Gran."

I rolled my eyes. I preferred Gran.

"I saw that," said Heart, without looking up. She began chopping the celery and onions. "Grandmother Sylvia refused to come to Whispering Spirit Farm when we lived there. I heard Larry tell Evie once that Grandmother's exact words were, 'I'd rather be dead than consort with Communists.' The only time Grandmother has visited Gabriel's Garden was when you were in India at that ashram meditating with Guru Bobolink."

"Bobistani," I corrected.

"You know, you'd probably still be there if Tum hadn't hauled you back."

That year in India I was hiding from everyone, including myself. I'd arrived at Guru Bobistani's broken, and it had taken a long time to piece myself together, long hours of chanting and meditation, of searching my soul for any glimmer of goodness. And I'm not sure that you can ever truly reweave all the remnants when you shatter a life, even if by accident. "You break it, you bought it," takes on a whole new karmic meaning when you kill someone.

"Another year with Bobolink and you would have ended up wandering the continents barefoot, a bag of bones with a shaved head and a dirty yoga mat strapped to your back." Heart shuddered.

"That was the guy on *Kung Fu*," I corrected my sister.

"There but for the grace of Spirit," my practical sister said.

Still, I wanted to know more about my grandmother.

Something didn't add up in this house of numbers. Evie had designed her octagonal home according to the principles of sacred mathematics, which has at its root the study of nature. My mother believes that the universe was created by geometric plan, that the honeybee constructs its hexagonal cells not just because it's an efficient way to hold honey but because it brings balance and harmony to the bees' work.

I have always felt a natural serenity here in the house that Evie built—until now.

My grandmother's unsettling presence had planted all sorts of questions in my mind. I pressed Heart for answers. "Why didn't I know about this missing branch of the family tree?"

"You never asked."

"Why would I?" I said. "There are no photos of her or any of the grandparents around. I thought they were all dead." Another thought struck. "There aren't more relatives to spring out of the bushes and surprise me, are there? Crazy extended family members that show up at Thanksgiving or crash Christmas?"

I searched my mind for bits of conversation, for familial references and anecdotes about Uncle Herman who escaped some prison camp using nothing but his shoelaces or Aunt Eloise the Hoarder. Nothing.

"No, Maya," Heart said. "Evie's parents are dead, and Grandfather Lawrence is gone, too. He was a lawyer. Both Larry and Evie were only children."

"Where does Grandmother live?" I asked, removing the pan of rolls from the oven.

"Seattle, I believe," said Heart, plucking hot rolls from the pan and tossing them into a basket.

A desperate Larry called from the other room, "Time to eat?"

At the table, Evie faced off with Grandmother, each occupying an end seat. Larry took the chair next to Evie. Heart, David, and Sadie occupied one side of the table; I pulled out the chair between Grandmother and Larry on the other side. It was a large table, and I had seldom seen it set so formally with a damask tablecloth, linen napkins, and an abundance of forks and crystal. There were even candles and a centerpiece, flowers Sadie had collected from Evie's garden. Centerpieces were reserved for holidays and special events in our family. I assumed this display of civilized elegance was for Grandmother, who was the type to make you think twice about resting your elbows on the table. I wondered: How had my casually inclined father ever survived in her home?

We all picked up our salad forks, except Grandmother. "No grace, Lawrence?" she asked.

Everyone froze, forks in mid-air. All eyes turned to Larry, who slowly lowered his offending utensil. We all followed suit as Larry mumbled, "Why don't you lead us, Mother?"

With a nod, Grandmother looked each of us in the eye until we all bowed our heads, then started in, "Bless this food we are about to eat . . ."

When she finished with an "amen," air rushed back into the room, cutlery clanged again, and serving dishes were passed. I heard Heart shush Sadie when she asked the meaning of "grace."

"I'll explain later," Heart whispered.

But that wasn't the only question on Sadie's mind. She was trying to wrap her head around someone so old being related to her. "So you are my *great*-grandmother?" she asked, ignoring the chicken, mashed potatoes, and green beans on her plate. "I'm eight. How old are you?"

David tapped his daughter's shoulder and motioned for her to start eating. "It's not polite to ask someone's age."

"Why not? People are always asking my age. Is this age discrimination?"

Heart frowned. "Where did you hear about age discrimination?"

"A lady at the grocery store said she could run items over the scanner faster than the clerk, but they wouldn't hire her because she's old and there's age discrimination."

Grandmother was watching Sadie with a look that somehow found Heart at fault. She told my sister, "As I used to tell Lawrence, precocious children are like puppies—only cute for so long."

Heart snapped straighter in her chair. It was never wise to mess with Heart's Mother Spirit, as I called it. Her eyes took on a sharp look, and I wondered if I should relieve her of the knife she was clutching. I glanced at Evie, who also seemed about to leap over the centerpiece with talons bared. This surprised me since my calm mother did not fly into battle. Maybe Larry should move the wine bottle. I decided to rescue Grandmother with a deft change of subject.

I quickly cleared my throat and said, "Gran, I'm just back from Paris. Have you ever been there?"

Grandmother's eyes widened. She didn't know whether

to correct my use of such a familiar form of address or answer my question. Finally, picking up her fork and delicately spearing a green bean, she said, "A ghastly city if ever there was one."

Sadie, oblivious to the vibes swirling around the table, said, "I love all things French. Croissants. Berets. The Eiffel Tower. The word *bonsoir*." She drew this last out in a romantic sigh. "There are fountains everywhere, and people even as old as you ride around on bicycles."

Heart and Sadie watched a lot of Audrey Hepburn movies, *Funny Face* being one of their favorites.

Ignoring Sadie, Grandmother asked me, "Why were you in that filthy city?"

"I was looking for someone," I said. "A man who went missing in Afghanistan."

"If he disappeared in the Middle East, why on earth would you look for him in Paris?" Grandmother's tone of voice made it sound as if I were geographically challenged.

"We met with his family, hoping they'd heard from him," I explained, "but they weren't helpful. There'd been an estrangement. They were quite upset."

Grandmother looked straight at my father and said, "I know how they feel."

From there, the conversation circled the table, with Grandmother playing the hostess. Skipping Sadie, she made a point of speaking to everyone, asking questions to draw us out and showing that someone had been keeping her informed of family news. She served compliments with a tart tongue: "Selling many toys, Lawrence?" "Your home looks nice, Evangeline, but eight sides. Goodness, don't you find all these angles difficult when it comes to decorating?" "David, are you still a gardener?" "Heart, this salad is so fresh and green."

When it came to my turn, I waited to see what short-coming Grandmother would come up with. She didn't disappoint. "So, Maya, this yoga studio you run, what de-nomination is it?"

"Yoga is nondenominational, Gran," I said, fitting an elbow on the table and waving a roll in my grandmother's direction. "My students are all ages, from all walks of life, Catholics to atheists, I imagine. I'm not sure about the athe-ist; I'm only guessing."

Grandmother frowned at my elbow. "But don't the things you teach conflict?"

"I teach the importance of balance in all parts of life."

"Balance." Grandmother wrinkled her nose. "What a namby-pamby dogma. The care of the soul is not for sissies, young lady."

"Now, we get to the reason she's here," Evie whispered to Larry. Larry looked worried.

Grandmother continued, "I believe in the word of the Lord. *That* is my religion. Never go anywhere without the Holy Bible."

I thought of Ida at Whispering Spirit Farm bent over her Bible every morning. "I bet you consult it every day," I said.

"Sometimes more than once a day, depending on how many trying people I have to deal with." Grandmother pat-ted her napkin against her frowning lips.

"So the Good Book brought you here?" asked Larry.

"And the tent revival at the Chapel of the Forgiving Heart. Know the place?"

Evie exchanged a glance with me and reached for her wineglass. My grandmother was marching right into the suspect arms of the Reverend Harold Miley.

Larry said, "Not again, Mother. What is this—your third revival this year?"

"I like them. Gets me out of the house."

Larry shook his head in disgust. "These religious hootenannies are always out in some field where a woman your age has no business being. You could fall and break a hip."

"I always take an escort, Lawrence."

"So who's your escort this time?"

"You are, Lawrence."

Larry's fork dropped, as did the jaws of several at the table. Evie choked on her wine.

Grandmother saluted Larry with her glass of water. "I am a warrior of the Lord, Lawrence. I go where I am called, and this time so do you."

Having recovered my ability to speak, I leaned forward. "Called?"

"Yes, called, young lady. I know you might find that hard to believe—"

"Not at all," I said, thinking of the shaman's diary sitting in the safe in my apartment. "I believe very much in callings."

As Heart and I cleared the dishes, my phone chimed. It was a text from Jorn: *Got another message.*

CHAPTER 12

A PRICELESS PAIN IN THE NECK

LEAVING MY PARENTS TO my grandmother's mercy, I drove through the fading light to Jorn's house. As I approached his porch, I heard someone call my name. It was Jorn's next-door neighbor, Randy, the vague-but-sweet stoner and cactus drowner who sometimes watered Jorn's single plant. Randy took this job—keeping alive a tiny zebra cactus named Armadillo—seriously. Leaning over the banister of his porch, Randy called, "*Namaste*, Maya." Randy came to yoga when he remembered the schedule and where the studio was, which was not often.

I waved to Randy and knocked on the red door to Jorn's small Craftsman-style bungalow. When I heard, "Come in,"

I stepped inside. The place was in its usual state of disarray. Passing the fireplace mantel, I saw a half-eaten, dried peanut butter sandwich without the jelly; a pile of change; and a tiny plastic action hero. Jorn, an occasional geocacher, used an app on his phone to follow coordinates to treasure hidden by other geocachers. The treasure could contain anything from kids' toys to a packet of wildflower seeds to a limited edition geocoin. Jorn claimed it was good exercise for his stiff hip, but it also was about following a lead to the end of the story, a natural game for a seeker.

I picked up the sandwich with my fingertips and carried it through the dining room-turned-office and into Jorn's spotless kitchen, where I deposited it in the trash and said hello to Armadillo on the window sill. From upstairs, Jorn called, "Maya?"

I found him in the spare bedroom, which was stacked to the ceiling with moving boxes.

"What took you so long?" he growled.

"I was meeting my grandmother."

"Didn't know you had one."

"Neither did I."

He looked at me strangely.

"What?" I said. "I suppose you know all the limbs on your family tree."

"At least the important ones. Grandmothers are important."

"In my defense," I said, "I thought she was dead."

"There's a lot of that going around."

We had never discussed Jorn's family. I only knew what everyone in town knew—that he was the nephew of Al Jorn, longtime owner of the town newspaper, *The Independent*.

"So what's your family like?" I asked.

Jorn shrugged. "No parents, no grandparents, just Uncle Al and me and a few cousins I wouldn't recognize if my life depended on it. Oh, and my brother. The Jorns are like the bristlecone pines—half dead but still alive. It takes a lot to put us in the ground."

Some bristlecone pine trees are the oldest known individuals of any species on the planet, more than five thousand years old. Their wood is so durable that even when the tree dies, the wood doesn't rot; it erodes like stone from wind, rain, and freezing, which can take centuries. So, often one side of the tree is green with life, and the other is a wood sculpture slowly wearing away. I liked the idea of Jorn having such a durable lineage.

"Back up," I said. "A brother? Why have you never mentioned him?"

"We don't talk, text, or email." Jorn continued, "Al's the one who came and got me out of the hospital. Al took care of me. End of story." From the tone of his voice, it obviously was not.

Jorn shoved the topic of a thoughtless brother back in the closet and locked it away so quickly I didn't know what to say. "There's been a Jorn in journalism for generations," he said, "but I'm probably the last of the Jorns in the newspaper business now that Uncle Al is living the deadline-free life in sunny Florida."

"You don't think he's coming back?"

Jorn snorted. "He's traded his snow shovel for sunblock. Hell, he *gave* me the house along with the newspaper. I've got the paperwork to prove it. They're my babies now." Jorn did not sound like a happy parent.

"I guess I thought you'd go back to being a foreign correspondent."

Jorn didn't meet my eyes. "You have to be able to run fast in a war zone."

Was Jorn making excuses for not returning to his old life?

"Besides, Uncle Al believes this is a good place to hide out."

"Hide out?"

"He says if any insurgents come looking to finish the job, they'll surely stick out on the streets of Gabriel's Garden."

I surveyed the stacks of boxes. "It doesn't look like you plan on staying."

"I've been busy, Maya, and being around you hasn't exactly speeded up my recovery plan."

In addition to the injuries he received in Afghanistan, Jorn was healing from another bullet wound, and it was mostly—all right, completely—my fault. The Down Dog Diary was stolen a few months ago, and he was shot while helping me get it back. I had tried to make it up to him during his rehab. "I stocked your freezer with food and brought you books," I reminded him.

"Healthy food probably made by Heart and boring books."

The casseroles *were* made by Heart, but as for the reading material, I thought he would love books on politics and geography. The shelves downstairs were exploding with nonfiction. Not liking this feeling of guilt, I grumbled, "I don't know what you were doing trying to save me anyway. I can save myself."

A sly grin crept across his face. He knew I hated being in

his—or anyone's—debt. I was the child who played super-hero and rescued others. I was the woman who heard cries and rushed down a dark alley to save the day.

Turning back to the room of boxes, he eyed the mess and said, "I don't even think these are all mine."

"So why are we here?"

Jorn immediately sobered and pulled his phone from his pocket. With a tap he brought up a text message from Gasquet: *Where is it?*

"Where is what?"

"Damned if I know," Jorn said, "but if I've got something I don't know I have, it's probably in here."

WE SHUFFLED BOXES AROUND and pawed through them long into the night. Jorn was right; some of the boxes were his uncle's. They included archives of *The Independent*, going back fifty years or more, copies of the newspaper now shred-ded by the local mice and recycled into cozy nests. Al also had left behind his entire cache of Minnesota survival gear: parkas capable of taking on subzero temperatures, lug sole boots, multicolored wool scarves, hats with earflaps, gloves of varying thicknesses, and more snow scrapers than any one person will ever need.

Jorn examined each item, setting aside the hats, gloves, and scrapers to keep. "Could have used these last winter."

The boxes from Jorn's Washington apartment, still se-curely sealed by the movers, contained many items he hadn't seen since before he was injured. Jorn and Gasquet were am-bushed in late October. Jorn spent November and some of

December in hospitals, first in Germany and then in the States, moving to Gabriel's Garden shortly before Christmas to recuperate under the care of his uncle Al. I met Jorn the following February, when he limped into my studio with all the joy of a sulking teenager and said his doctor recommended yoga—of all things—if he ever wanted to move normally again.

While Jorn was in the hospital, Al had arranged for a service to pack up Jorn's belongings, close his apartment, and ship all his worldly possessions to Gabriel's Garden. The plan was for Jorn to stay with his uncle until he got back on his feet. Jorn wasn't quite sure how he ended up with a house and a newspaper in Minnesota and his uncle wound up with a margarita and a crossword puzzle in Florida. That conversation, probably conducted under heavy medication, was still hazy in his memory.

In Jorn's boxes were books and more books. I couldn't imagine where Jorn would put them. The shelves in the living room were already filled to the rafters. "Hey, here are my Harry Dresden books," he said, setting the urban fantasy series aside. Others joined the pile: political thrillers, biographies, mysteries, science fiction, Westerns. Westerns?

"I thought you were a just-the-facts-ma'am kind of reader," I said, referring to the nonfiction collection below.

"What?" Jorn looked up. "Oh, you mean the books downstairs? Those are Al's. He said he wasn't paying by the pound to move books to Florida. So I inherited them with the house."

"I don't know where you're going to put all these."

"There's always room for a good book."

I opened one box to find clothes. Another held glassware, shampoo, old magazines, and a remote control. "Give me that," he said, plucking the remote from my hand and adding it to a growing pile of items he wanted to keep.

At the bottom of a large box of towels, screwdrivers, bottles of over-the-counter medications, and a cereal bowl still containing the remains of Jorn's last breakfast in the apartment were a few letters and an unopened package. I pulled out the mail, thinking there might be unpaid bills to attend to, but it was the package that called to me. Sweeping my hand over the long box, I felt the hum of an unknown energy.

"Uh, Jorn," I said, looking up at him. He was holding a framed photo that had been carefully bubble-wrapped by the movers. It was of Jorn sitting on the ground, legs crossed, scribbling on a small pad of paper as a group of soldiers talked around a campfire. I knew by its distinctive composition that Gasquet had taken it. He placed it carefully on the "keep" pile.

I cleared my throat, drawing Jorn's attention, and handed him the package. From its size, it looked like it could hold a nice bottle of wine, perhaps French wine since the mailing label stated that it had originated in Paris.

"Paris?" Jorn frowned, ripping open the package and drawing out a hinged wooden box. There was no identification on the outside of the box. Carefully, he lifted the latch and opened the box. Nestled inside amid a burrow of padding was a small sculpture, not more than ten inches high, all smooth white curves—a choirboy in a robe, sad face turned to the side. The energy in the room changed; it felt like the energies in museums. I edged closer. Neither Jorn nor I wanted to lift the sculpture from the box.

Jorn read the short letter that came with the sculpture. It was from a law firm in France. "It says they were instructed to send this to me by their client Gasquet Dubois." He scanned the label on the package for a shipping date.

"Gasquet's last wish?" I asked.

"It must have arrived at my apartment while I was in the hospital."

"And your uber-efficient movers packed it up."

"Why not? Hell, they even packed my dirty underwear." He wrinkled his nose.

"Why did Gasquet send you this? Does this mean he's dead or alive?"

Jorn didn't answer. Instead, he asked, "Does this look familiar to you?"

I studied the sculpture. Suddenly, my mind flew back to the Minneapolis Institute of Art on the first day we saw Gasquet. My eyes widened. "It can't be."

"If it is, we've got trouble."

EVIE AND ROSELYN, THE town's art experts, stood beside the aquamarine table in Roselyn's sky blue kitchen, staring at the small sculpture with expressions that could only be described as enraptured. The silence in the blue house was almost reverent. Jorn and I, standing beside them, exchanged glances. After several moments, without taking her eyes off the sculpture, Evie whispered to Roselyn, "What do you think? Is it—"

"A tomb sculpture?" Roselyn said, leaning closer until she was practically nose to nose with the tiny choirboy. "It certainly looks like it."

Evie whistled. "Then it must be more than five hundred years old."

"And in perfection condition," Roselyn sighed.

Evie bent to get a closer look, too. "The craftsmanship is exquisite. It's like the stone is moving, swaying." She sounded envious.

"Emotion caught in alabaster," Roselyn agreed. Both women straightened.

"Don't you just want to touch it?" Evie groaned, her hands clamped to her sides. Roselyn nodded, although Evie didn't see. Both women were mesmerized. I had not often seen my mother so caught in a spell.

Jorn broke the moment of adoration. "Can you tell us more about it?"

Roselyn shook herself as if wakening from a trance and rushed to a bookshelf in the living room. She began pulling down books and tossing them on the coffee table. Dressed in a long tie-dyed skirt and tank top in her signature color, the Blue Lady knelt over the books, flipping through one and then the other. "Aha," she cried, pointing her paint-smudged finger in the air. She scrambled to her feet and carried a book over to Evie. Heads together, they leaned over the large art book.

"Well?" I nudged them.

"Sculptors Jean de la Huerta and Antoine le Moiturier spent twenty-seven years working on the tomb of John the Fearless," Roselyn read. "Effigies of the duke of Burgundy and his wife, Margaret of Bavaria, lie on top of the tomb. The tomb includes an extravagantly ornamental Gothic arcade with niches for a parade of individually sculpted tomb mourners, a funeral march in stone."

"Do you think this is authentic, a real Mourner, or a reproduction?" I asked.

Evie and Roselyn had no idea.

"It's got to be a reproduction," Jorn said.

"If not," Evie said, "it's priceless."

That thought sent unease shivering down my spine. It was my experience that priceless often meant pain in the neck.

Roselyn gasped, and we all turned to her. She was reading the art book again. "It says during the French Revolution, the tomb was disassembled and partly destroyed. When it was restored and placed in the Musée des Beaux-Arts de Dijon, not all of the forty Mourners were recovered. Three Mourners from the tomb of John the Fearless are owned by other museums." She paused. "And one has yet to be found."

We all gaped at the small figure that until recently had been sharing a mover's box with old breakfast cereal.

"Oh shit," groaned Jorn.

CHAPTER 13

IN THE REDEMPTION BUSINESS

D ON'T GET ME WRONG. I love churches; it's the people inside them that test my dedication to a peaceful existence. I respect holy places, corners of the world that have absorbed prayers and invocations. I believe those drowning in despair and those floating with gratitude leave something of themselves behind. To me, such places are Grand Central Stations of energy—they make me feel fully alive and deeply calm at the same time. So, when my grandmother announced that she wished to attend a Sunday church service and expected someone to drive her, I volunteered. Besides, I wanted another shot at the Reverend Harold Miley.

I arrived at my parents' house promptly at nine thirty on

Sunday morning. Grandmother had insisted I be on time. She was wearing one of her Chanel summer suits and nylons; I was wearing jeans. She took one look at my attire and said, "So they have casual Sundays in Minnesota?"

"Don't shoot the chauffeur," I said, tucking her into the passenger seat and helping her with the shoulder harness.

With a frown, Grandmother settled her handbag on her lap and adjusted the pillbox hat on her head. I gave a tug to my baseball cap, got in, and pulled out of the drive.

My grandmother smelled of lilacs, an old-fashioned scent that I liked. She was quiet as we drove, and I wondered if she had already started her prayers. The Chapel of the Forgiving Heart was about ten miles out of town, a stretch Tessa made every day on her bike to visit Olivia or to attend yoga. I worried about Tessa and Olivia riding their bikes on this two-lane road with narrow shoulders. Tessa had not been to yoga in the two weeks since Val crashed my class, and I wanted to check on her.

Already the day was heating up so I kept the windows closed and the air conditioner on high to keep Grandmother from melting in all that couture—even though she did not seem the type to sweat. I cast a glance toward her solemn profile and realized the shape of her nose was the shape of my nose and Larry's. It was a nose that poked itself into other people's business (as I often did), that tracked a cyber scent in Larry's den of computers, and that, I had a feeling, had brought my grandmother to town. Something was in the wind, and Gran had followed it here.

"Do you often pop up in places without warning?" I asked. Startled out of her reverie, Grandmother tensed but kept her attention on the passing landscape. "I emailed Lawrence that I was coming. Obviously, he either didn't believe me or he chose not to pass on the information for fear of upsetting Evangeline."

"Why would Evie be upset?"

"I haven't a clue." Grandmother stared out the window at the fields of sunflowers. After a long pause, she mumbled, "After all, she *did* win."

"Win?"

"Lawrence."

Her single response, still tinged with disappointment after all these years, surprised me. How could anyone be jealous of Evie and her loving spirit? I tried to imagine the battle of these two women over my free-spirited father. How had my dove of a mother vanquished this hawk of stubborn conviction?

The problem with competition is that we spend all of our thought on what will be, instead of living what is. I frequently see this in my students. They are impatient for progress: When will I be able to do the Crow? they ask. I tell them that yoga is not about competition. It does not matter how many years it takes to accomplish the Crow Pose or if they ever do. It is the practice that matters, not reaching the finish line. But we are a results-oriented culture.

"Gran, have you ever heard of *santosha*?" I flicked her a glance. "It's one of the *niyamas* of yoga."

"What on earth is a *niyama*?"

"*Niyamas* are inner disciplines, how we treat ourselves. They are sometimes called observances, or the 'thou shalts' of yoga."

Grandmother turned to me and said, "I have the Ten Commandments to take care of that department."

I nodded. "There are only five *niyamas*, and one is *santosha* or contentment. Thou shalt be at peace with what happens. We cultivate contentment and tranquility by finding happiness with what we have and who we are—regardless of circumstances."

Grandmother's gaze shifted back to the front of the car, her focus on the road ahead. "I am quite content as I am, Maya, without all that yamaha stuff."

But was she? While her energy appeared composed, I felt an unhappy tension in my grandmother. What was she really searching for in Gabriel's Garden?

At the Chapel of the Forgiving Heart, we parked in the mown field alongside about a dozen other cars. Even though she didn't like it, I helped my independent grandmother out of the car and insisted on keeping a hand on her elbow as we crossed the rough ground.

Once we reached the sidewalk in front of the chapel, Grandmother stopped and took in the small country church with its arched windows and its plain cross atop the gabled double doors. The red doors stood open—welcoming arms or an invitation into the Reverend Miley's web. She read the sign about the tent revival. New information had been added in red paint at the top of the banner: "With Exciting Special Guest: Sister MJ."

What Grandmother Sylvia saw satisfied her, and with a nod and no help from me, she mounted the steps. It was gloomy inside the chapel and muggy, the only breeze coming from the open doors. There were maybe twenty people scattered throughout the chapel, several fanning themselves with cardboard fans from a collection at the back of the church. The Reverend Miley had obviously made a foray on the booths at the Minnesota State Fair, which was held every year at the end of summer in sultry Saint Paul and was the region's premiere source for free promotional fans. I grabbed two, one selling mortuary services (I gave this one to Grandmother) and one advertising season tickets to the Minnesota Twins.

Grandmother slid into a worn wooden pew about midway down the center aisle, and I sat beside her. I spotted Tessa in the front pew, looking lovely and reverent in a flowered summer dress; her long brown hair pulled back from her face with a butterfly clip. Val sat next to her in a clean, short-sleeved white shirt, no tie. The organ music was recorded and traditional. No Dolly Parton warbled from the speakers today. When the smiling Reverend Harold Miley bounced up the steps to the pulpit in the same old suit and tails, I slid down in my seat and crossed my arms.

The ten o'clock service lasted two hours. With my backside growing increasingly numb, I prayed every "amen" would be the last one. While the congregation wilted under the heat and close confines of the airless church, the preacher's intensity never waned. He pontificated on a number of pits waiting for the unsuspecting or the dark-hearted: having sex without marriage, being lazy, putting oneself above the Almighty. He touched on everything but double parking. When he started on worshipping false gods, he caught my eye. I smiled at him.

The preacher's rants were punctuated with song, hymns I

didn't know, led with exuberance by the music-loving minister. The Reverend Miley was God's aging cheerleader who believed in passing the hat not once, but twice, and each time my grandmother placed a one-hundred-dollar bill in the basket. I kept watch over my grandmother throughout the service, worried that the heat would overpower the capacity of our flimsy fans. Several times during the torture session, I directed my fanning in her direction. That my self-reliant grandmother didn't tell me what to do with my fan was an indication, to me, that she was feeling the drain of the heat. When the final "amen" rang from the rafters, I jumped to my feet and helped my stiff grandmother to hers.

Everyone filed out into the bright day through the front doors, where the Reverend Miley waited like a spider. He latched on to each soul leaving the chapel, shaking hands and whispering support. When it was our turn, I introduced the minister to my grandmother.

He leaned conspiratorially toward Grandmother, favoring her with an unctuous smile, and said, "I've been wanting to get your granddaughter here."

"I have my own places of worship, Reverend," I said, "and they're a heck of a lot cooler."

The Reverend Harold Miley laughed.

"Fine words today, Reverend," said Grandmother, who had pulled a white lace-trimmed handkerchief from her purse and was dabbing at her upper lip. "Although I thought you took some liberties with the Good Book."

"Ah, a purist." The reverend winked at my grandmother. "I feel it is my job to interpret for my congregation on occasion."

"Really." Grandmother's tone indicated she did not entirely approve of such license.

"I am delighted to have a true believer in our midst. I expect you will keep me on the straight and narrow, Mrs. Skye. While you're here, I hope you come to the revival," he said, patting her arm, a presumptuous gesture that ruffled my grandmother's feathers.

In a voice that would have had schoolchildren straightening in their seats, Grandmother said, "I wouldn't miss it."

The Reverend Miley's face lit up. "I'm extremely excited about the late addition of Sister MJ. She's a stirring speaker."

I had never heard of Sister MJ, but apparently my grandmother had. "Quite a coup to get such an international presence at a small revival."

"The hand of God," the reverend said, nodding toward the heavens. "I nearly fell over when her camp called to offer her services, free of charge. Apparently, she will be in the Twin Cities at the same time as the revival. I'm sure she'll draw a crowd."

Grandmother's response was the lift of a brow.

As we walked to the car, I asked my grandmother, "Do you know Sister MJ?"

"Everyone knows Sister MJ," she muttered. "She eats liberty-taking preachers like him for breakfast."

Hiding a smile, I asked Grandmother to wait in the car for a moment. "I just want to say hello to a friend. I won't be long," I promised. She nodded and sighed as she slid into the soft cushion of the car seat.

I searched the groups forming and reforming on the church lawn, greeting each other, sharing news. Finally, I saw Tessa near the side of the church. She was looking at me. I walked over to her.

"Are you doing okay? You haven't been to yoga in a while."

Tessa shrugged and smoothed the skirt of her dress. "I'll be coming back." The determination in her voice lifted me.

"I've tried talking to your dad. I didn't want to cause you trouble, but—"

Suddenly, Valmer rounded the corner of the church and headed for us. "What are you doing, Tessa?" he demanded.

"We're just talking, Val," Tessa said, exasperation in her voice. She seemed more perturbed by the interruption than afraid of her brother.

He spoke to me for the first time. "If you care about Tessa, you'll leave her alone. You're just confusing her."

Tessa threw up her arms. "I can make my own decisions, Val."

After a hard look at me, Val turned to go, but I stopped him. "One more thing, Val. Don't ever bring a gun into my studio again," I said in a deadly voice.

Val's jaw worked and his fists clenched. For several moments, we traded stony glares then, with a glance at his sister, he left.

On the ride home, Grandmother aired a list of the Reverend Miley's inaccuracies and faulty logic. "So, does this mean you aren't going to the tent revival?" I asked. "I mean, it sounds to me like the guy doesn't know his stuff."

"Oh, I'll be there. To keep the Reverend Miley on his toes. And I wouldn't miss Sister MJ."

When I pulled up to my parents' house and began to get out of the car, my grandmother laid a hand on my arm to stop me.

"What is it, Gran?"

Grandmother Sylvia began searching through her leather handbag. Finally, she pulled out another handkerchief, this one embroidered with purple flowers in one corner. Wrapped in the white handkerchief was a tiny, liquid-filled bottle with a cork. She looked at me with worried eyes.

"Maya, I want you to take care of this. This is important. I was told to give it to you."

"Told?"

"God told me you would need this." With care, she placed the bottle and handkerchief in my hand. The bottle hung from a silver chain. "I've carried this in my purse for a long time," she said, words softened with memory.

"What is it?" I whispered.

"Sacred oil. Blessed. If you or someone you know needs healing, place a drop on the handkerchief and press it to the person's heart."

I didn't know what to say. I tried to smile at her with reassurance. "Nothing is going to happen, Gran."

Grandmother brushed my words aside, unclipped her seat belt, and reached for the door handle. "Take care of that. You're going to need it." She opened the door then looked back at me. "And I want it back when you're done."

CHAPTER 14

FLY BLACKBIRD EYES

TESSA CAME TO MONDAY yoga class with a black eye. I tried to focus on keeping my energy loving and compassionate, but the sight of Tessa's swollen face tapped right into my core need to protect the weak, something I had been doing since I was a child in the commune. Although Gandhi insisted you could change the world without bloodying your fists, it just never seemed to turn out that way for me.

Jorn was upset about Tessa's condition as well. I could see him struggling more than usual, fighting the poses, holding his breath.

"Breathe," I reminded the class as well as myself.

In the center of the room, Olivia on her orange-red mat covered in tropical flowers and Tessa on a purple mat borrowed from the studio acted as if nothing had happened.

They smiled at each other and whispered. When Olivia fell out of Crow Pose for the third time, I saw a grinning Tessa help her back into it, balancing Olivia's knees on her bent arms. Then Tessa returned to her own mat and lifted herself into the difficult inverted pose.

The Crow Pose, in which the entire body is curled and balanced on the arms as if it is ready to take flight, signifies transcendence. I told the class, "Black crows, the messengers of the gods, visited the first Dalai Lama when he was born. Because they can fly, crows break the chains of the mortal world and soar into the heavens. To be the crow, you must learn to trust yourself."

"I'm afraid I'm going to fall on my face," grunted a flushed Julia Lune, holding her breath in intense concentration.

"Breathe," I repeated. "Trust your inner strength. Ultimately, the Crow is designed to teach us to listen to our inner voice, our intuition. Break the chain of what you believe you can do, and you will rise above your limitations."

But as the class wore on, rising above it all became increasingly difficult. The more balanced Tessa became, the more distracted Jorn and I became. At the end of the class, we shared a look and both rose from Corpse Pose with the same intention. We approached the girls, who were kneeling on the floor, chattering and rolling up their mats. Olivia said something that made Tessa laugh. I winced in sympathy for Tessa's puffy eye.

"Olivia, Tessa. Can we talk?" I asked, sitting on the floor beside them. They stopped rolling their mats and peered at me. I pointed to my own eye and asked Tessa, "How'd that happen?"

She shrugged. "I fell."

The obvious lie disappointed me. "Come on," I said with a sigh, but Tessa didn't blink.

I had to ask. "Tessa, do you feel safe?"

"Yes." Her eyes dared me to take it further.

"How is that possible?"

Tessa reached up with both hands and pulled her ponytail tighter then went back to rolling her mat. "It was an accident. No big deal."

Olivia twisted the pink braid in her hair. "Tess, maybe you should—"

Tessa cut her off. "I got it."

"But—"

"No, Liv."

Jorn, who had been standing to the side, tapped my shoulder and bade me follow him over to the Buddha table.

"Don't push it," he said in a lowered voice.

"She's a human punching bag!" I whispered fiercely.

"She's stronger than you think."

I knew he was right. Tessa was an old soul, one who seemed to have been born with the wisdom of the world already in her heart. I blew my bangs off my face in frustration. "But—"

Studying his bare feet, Jorn said, "Sometimes we do things that make *us* feel better, but that don't actually help the other person."

I hated it when Jorn turned guru on me, when I had to admit he was right and I was wrong.

I walked out of the studio, went up to my bedroom, and searched through the bathroom drawers for the cosmetic concealer Heart had once bought me. My sister had no qualms about letting me know when I looked like something the cat had dragged in.

As Olivia and Tessa got on their bikes, I handed Tessa the concealer. "This'll tone down the colors."

Tessa's eyes widened in surprise. "Thanks."

"*Namaste*," I said.

I watched them pedal off in the direction of Olivia's house. Jorn gave me a friendly nudge as he passed me, his version of a pat on the head for doing the right thing, then climbed into his Jeep.

Back in the studio, alone, I sat in meditation, seeking the emptiness where answers lived. My breath became one with the breath of the trees, the birds in the sky, the deer in the woods, the dolphins in the sea. Everything faded away. And when I surfaced, I was as lost as I had been when I began. Sometimes, it was like that. Answers were like babies; they arrived in their own time.

I stretched, rose, and started the tai chi forms Tum had taught me. Tingling energy flowed like invisible waters from one hand to the other. Parting the Wild Horse's Mane. White Crane Flashes Wings. Stroking the Bird's Tail. Such beautiful names for lethalness.

I once asked a fellow tai chi student if she could protect herself with her tai chi. She laughed and said, "Only if my attacker moves in slow motion."

I didn't tell her that, in my experience, Stroking the Bird's Tail can cause considerable damage when applied at the right moment to the right opponent.

In the empty yoga studio, filled with sadness for one of

my students, I kicked, parried, punched—and tried not to picture my invisible foe with the military flat-top, the edgy temper, and the muscular arms of Tessa's brother.

THAT EVENING JORN AND I met with Julia Lune and her husband, Jean-Luc Dornier. Julia Lune was the pen name of the town's celebrity romance writer. A regular in my yoga classes, she was a pleasantly plump bird in vivid colors, a woman of Russian descent who usually brought a fun vibe to class even as she groaned through the poses. I could always tell when the plot of her latest romance novel wasn't cooperating. At those times, Julia became quieter and fell out of her poses more often.

Her French lawyer husband was devoted to her and not in the least jealous that Julia spent her days dreaming of ways to lure other men down the rocky road to love. "Research," Jean-Luc says of the photos of bare-chested, drool-worthy men Julia rips from magazines and pins to the wall of her office. "They can have Julia's books. I have Julia."

Julia welcomed us with a glass of wine and led us to a patio that was better equipped than some kitchens, with a tall stone fireplace and a grill that Jorn eyed with envy. Behind us, two stories of glass and wood rose in a modern ark of a house. Jean-Luc's baby grand piano sat in the corner of the living room with an excellent view of the Dorniers' private lake.

Jorn and I sank into the thick cushions of two wicker chairs and just sat there for a moment, absorbing the evening quiet. The Minnesota night air sighed. It wouldn't be dark for another hour, plenty of time for the leggy herons to hunt their last meals of the day while the frogs sang.

Settling on the sofa next to her husband, Julia said, "About that girl Tessa. Is everything okay there?" Julia had been in yoga class today, her Gibson Girl bun askew and her glasses sliding down her nose as she struggled with Crow.

"She says she's okay."

Julia nodded. "But you'll keep an eye out?"

"You bet." Julia and I shared a look of understanding.

I've always been someone people turned to in times of trouble. I think it's my air of competence, the assurance that I will get things done, no matter what. I get that from Larry, who has no small amount of the fixer gene. But I think the Down Dog Diary is changing me even more so. It seems others, like Julia, can sense that I am the keeper, the healer. Each day, I learn more about the weight of the load Tum has passed to me.

Jorn had asked Jean-Luc to use his connections in France to find out more about the Paris law firm that had sent him the Mourner sculpture, which, for the time being, was residing in my new safe. Although it still made me nervous, I was growing accustomed to being responsible for valuable things like shamans' diaries and medieval art. And I knew Jorn's house was far from burglar proof. Hadn't I, then a complete stranger, talked Randy into fetching his spare key to Jorn's house and letting me snoop around when Jorn was in New Mexico? Jorn's forgetful neighbor kept the key attached to a hubcap, which was clearly marked "Peter's house."

Jorn showed Julia the photo of the tomb sculpture that he had sent earlier to Jean-Luc's email.

"It's beautiful," she said with a note of appreciation.

"Exquisite," agreed Jean-Luc, leaning back and settling his arm along the back of the sofa. Julia nestled against him, pushing up her round, chocolate-smudged glasses. Breathing in the scent of her hair, Jean-Luc's eyes softened behind his own clean, semi-rimless Armani style of eyewear. Observing them cuddle was like *GQ* meets Harry Potter. Cute.

"Paris is seven hours ahead of us. I reached one of the partners at the firm about three o'clock today, Paris time," said Jean-Luc with the slightest of accents. "He would not reveal how long Gasquet Dubois had been a client or when he last heard from Gasquet. This is an old Parisian firm, quite established and resolute in maintaining the confidentiality of its clients. It has kept the secrets of kings and financiers for generations."

"Do you know if the firm handles the affairs of the entire Dubois family?" Jorn asked.

"He would not say, but I got that impression."

"And yet they sent the sculpture to me instead of to Gasquet's family."

"I identified myself as your legal representative in the States and said I simply wanted to clarify why the 'package' was sent to you."

"And?"

"Apparently, Gasquet Dubois had set up instructions that were to be followed if he did not make his regular contact with the firm."

"Regular contact?" Jorn was puzzled.

Jean-Luc's fingers absently massaged the back of his wife's

neck as he spoke. "Monsieur Dubois called or texted at designated times. If he missed a specified number of appointed communications, certain actions were set in motion. One being the delivery to you of a package that had been secured in the firm's vault."

Jorn shook his head in disbelief. "In a crazy way, that sounds just like Gasquet. Orderly."

I asked, "Did his lawyer know the contents of the package?"

"*Non.*" Jean-Luc gave a shrug that upped his sophistication factor to 110 percent French. Julia and I grinned at each other. "And I did not tell him."

I leaned forward. "But wouldn't Gasquet's instructions trigger other actions, such as sending letters to the Dubois family?"

"I would think so," Jean-Luc said.

I thought this was highly likely as well. We'd seen how organized Gasquet was at his apartment. I was not surprised that he had planned for his demise, which is what it was looking like to me. And if Gasquet's family had received some "final words" from their son and brother, why did they still think he was alive?

Still, Jorn wasn't ready to bury Gasquet yet. "This doesn't prove Gasquet is dead," Jorn insisted. "It just means he couldn't communicate."

Jean-Luc looked intrigued. "What circumstances could account for that?"

"Lots of things in that part of the world," Jorn said. "Capture. Injury. Being lost in the mountains. No access to a phone. He could be lying in some villager's home, delirious, or with an injury that prevents him from remembering. He may not know who he is."

"Amnesia is not as common as romance novels would have us believe," said Julia. "In reality, it's fairly rare."

As we left, Jean-Luc kissed me on both cheeks, and Julia gave me a hug. Jorn thanked Jean-Luc.

"*Il n'y a pas de quoi*," Jean-Luc smiled. It was nothing.

With an arm wrapped around Julia's waist, Jean-Luc led his wife back into their contemporary house of glass, and Jorn walked me to my car. Opening the door for me, he paused, "You've got that look. What are you up to?"

I tried to appear innocent, but Jorn knew me too well. He leaned against the car, willing to wait me out.

Finally, I let out a sigh, opened the car door, and said, "I'm just going to pay the reverend a friendly visit."

"In the dead of night? You're hoping to catch the Reverend Miley off guard."

"I'm checking on one of my students."

Jorn shook his head, closed the door, and walked around the car. He pulled open the passenger door and plopped into the seat.

"You don't have to come with me," I said, starting the engine.

"Got nothing better to do." He leaned back in the seat and crossed his arms over his chest. "Just don't get me shot this time."

CHAPTER 15

KILLING GHOSTS

THE NIGHT WAS IMPENETRABLE in the country, far from the glow of the Twin Cities and the few streetlights of Gabriel's Garden. I nearly missed the turn-off for the Chapel of the Forgiving Heart. As I hit the brakes, the car that had been behind us ever since we left Gabriel's Garden slowed, honked, then gunned around us on the right. In the dark lane to the chapel, the gravel under my tires sounded too loud, which was a ridiculous thought to have passed through my mind. I wasn't trying to sneak up on the Reverend Harold Miley.

I steered around the church and followed a narrow road through the trees, the path I'd seen the crow take on my first visit here. The road dead-ended in a clearing that contained a small white farmhouse, a shed, and an old pickup—none in pristine condition. A light attached to a tall pole in the yard lit the clearing like a spotlight in the big top.

Jorn and I crossed the bright clearing, but before we could climb the porch steps and bang on the door, the Reverend Miley stepped out, dressed in a white T-shirt and trousers held up with black suspenders. The screen door shut firmly behind him.

With a smile, he looked down at us from the top of the steps and said, "Why, Miss Skye, bit late to come calling, isn't it? Or perhaps you need my spiritual assistance?"

As if I would ever come to him for help.

"Reverend," I said, "Tessa has a black eye."

The preacher crossed his arms over his chest. "How do you know that? Has she been to your class again?"

A curtain moved at the front window, and I caught a glimpse of Tessa's expressionless face.

"I saw her around town," I said. "Where I saw her is not the point. The condition I saw her in is."

The reverend turned his attention toward Jorn. Jorn nodded and introduced himself. "I'm Peter Jorn, Reverend. I publish *The Independent*."

The Reverend Miley raised an eyebrow. "Is this a matter for the newspaper?"

Jorn shook his head. "Not at the moment, Reverend."

The Reverend Miley's face filled with suspicion. He looked from Jorn to me. "What do you mean?"

I drew myself up and asked the Spirit for patience. "We just want to make sure Tessa is safe."

"Safe? Of course, my daughter's safe. Thank the Lord."

"The Lord didn't give her that shiner, Reverend," I said.

"You think I did?" His breath exploded from his chest. "I would never harm my daughter!"

"Can you say the same of Val?"

The preacher began to come down the steps toward us. Jorn tugged me quietly to his side. "Valmer is a loving brother, a good son, a decorated veteran. He would never—"

The minister's words were cut off by the boom of a gunshot echoing in the night. Jorn and I whirled and searched the darkness crowding the edges of the clearing. There was a rustle in the undergrowth and out stepped Val holding a gun.

For a moment, none of us said anything, then Jorn whispered in my ear, "Shotgun, twelve gauge, pump action. Not some farmer's old hunting rifle." I got the warning. A serious weapon. Jorn tried to push me behind him, but I wasn't one to hide. I slid a little to the right so I had a clear view of Val, who had stopped just inside the lit yard, a good sixty feet from us.

He stood, calm but tense, dressed for war in a black T-shirt and camo pants. "Pa? What're they doing here?"

"Nothing, Val. They were just leaving."

Val held the shotgun across his chest, his finger on the trigger. Without a word, he swung it toward us, and my heart skipped a beat. The air in the clearing changed. Keeping a grip on my arm, Jorn nudged me to start edging back toward the car. I could feel the reverend watching us. Val and I didn't take our eyes off each other. Suddenly, there was a movement in the woods to our right and a thrashing sound. Val whirled, dropped to one knee, and started firing. A roar of spitting buckshot ripped leaves from the trees and snapped off branches. I couldn't help it; I slapped my hands over my ears. Jorn drove me to the ground, his body landing on mine. When Val stopped shooting, heavy silence and the smell of gunpowder filled the clearing. Jorn and I looked up, first at Val who was tensely scanning the woods, and then at the woods themselves.

"Val!" screamed the reverend and Tessa at the same time.

I turned and saw Tessa slamming out of the front door and running toward her brother. The reverend made a grab for his daughter but missed. I struggled against Jorn, but he wouldn't let me up. I was terrified Val would turn his gun and shoot before realizing who his target was.

"Tessa!" I shouted, reaching a hand toward her.

But she only had eyes for her brother.

As she neared Val, Tessa slowed, stepping with caution. "Val, it's Tess." He didn't seem to hear her. He continued to clutch the gun and scan the perimeter. She edged closer. I heard her say in a low voice, "Val, it's okay. Everything's okay."

After several tense moments, Val looked up at his sister, and in the spotlight I saw the bewildered expression on his face.

"Tess?"

"Yes."

"Did we get 'em?"

After a pause, she said, "Yeah. We got 'em, Val."

She lifted the gun from his hands as if she'd done it a hundred times before and helped him to his feet.

As she guided her brother past us, Tessa looked at me, her eyes filled with remorse. Was it for her damaged brother or for Jorn and me being caught in the midst of her family's troubles? When the screen door shut behind Tessa and Val, the Reverend Harold Miley gave us a long look then followed his children inside.

Jorn and I got up. We were both shaking, the adrenaline pulsing through our veins. We turned toward the car with the same thought. No way were we leaving with someone possibly injured out there.

"Flashlight in the glove box?" he asked. I nodded.

Armed with the flashlight, we turned toward the dark woods. Our steps were quiet as we crossed the clearing. I prayed to Spirit that death was not waiting for us. After searching the heavy undergrowth, stepping over broken limbs and pushing dangling foliage aside, Jorn said, "Must have been an animal."

"Then where's the body?" I asked. "How could anything survive that barrage?"

Jorn squatted and studied a matted down area behind a large log. "Something took cover here. There's no way to tell if it was tonight. Could easily have been made days ago by sleeping deer."

"Blood?" I asked.

Jorn scanned the light over the spot. "No blood."

He rose, his eyes searching the area again. "Odd that a man of God didn't make sure one of his fold wasn't out here bleeding to death, isn't it?"

"Makes you wonder just how often this happens," I said.

"Maybe the reverend is used to his kid killing ghosts in the dark."

"Still—"

"It also makes you wonder how often Tessa rescues her brother from his nightmares."

I didn't want to think about that. I peered into the darkness. If a member of the reverend's congregation had paid a nightly visit, we would have known. Thinking of the noisy gravel road and the quiet night, I asked, "Did you hear another car?"

Jorn shook his head.

We returned to my car and sat for a moment, then I started the engine and made a U-turn in the clearing. Halfway home, Jorn's phone pinged. He pulled it out of his pocket and sucked in a breath. It was Gasquet again. Jorn read the text to me: *Why didn't you save me?*

CHAPTER 16

REVELATIONS

THE LAST-MINUTE APPEARANCE OF Sister MJ had turned a two-bit country church revival into a must-see event. It was five days before opening night on Monday, and already people were arriving. An enormous red-and-white striped tent had risen beside the Chapel of the Forgiving Heart. And from it spread a sea of small tents, pickups topped with campers, blimpy RVs, even tiny camp houses brought in on flatbed trucks. Campgrounds in nearby state parks hosted the overflow as did enterprising local farmers, who rented out space in their fields and offered to shuttle guests to the daily services. The Strawberry Bed & Breakfast in Gabriel's Garden was filled to its gingerbread-trimmed eaves.

I knew all of this because I had been keeping an eye on the Chapel of the Forgiving Heart and the preparations for the Reverend Miley's big show. I'd made secret visits to the growing make-shift community, making sure to dodge the minister and his son, whose job was to haul folding chairs into the tent. During each visit, I searched the faces I saw bent over barbecue grills, studying worn Bibles at camp tables, or smiling from lawn chairs next to RVs. I talked to people and showed them the photograph on my phone.

I searched for Gasquet. Not because I thought Gasquet was in need of a shot of faith, but because, based on his last message, I could only assume he was in the area and spying on us. And this was a perfect crowd to get lost in. I saw kids chasing each other under tent lines and around RVs, retired couples playing Cribbage, pet owners walking dogs—but no Gasquet.

Grandmother also was gearing up for the revival, spending hours in Evie's garden mumbling in prayer. One afternoon I watched her, sitting on a stone bench in one of her summer knit suits. You could tell it was a relaxed moment; she wasn't wearing a hat and she'd left the ubiquitous handbag in her room. Her eyes were closed. I stepped within ear shot and eavesdropped: "Well, Lord, I'm here, and I'm ready. If only you would tell me why—I know, I know. Not my place. But sometimes a person gets tired of following without question."

When a crow lit on the branch of a nearby maple tree and cawed loudly, Grandmother lifted her head and made a shooing motion. "Go away, disgusting bird." The crow retorted even more loudly, then, with a cock of its head toward me, flew over the treetops.

Grandmother returned to her conversation with God.

Peering down at her thin-skinned, veined hands, she fingered the thick platinum ring below one wrinkled knuckle, turning it again and again. It was her only jewelry except for the dignified pearls at her ears. Her nails were painted dusky pink, understated, proper, like my grandmother. She looked so fragile and so alone, and I felt the compulsion to go to her, to tell her about my life and ask about hers, but mostly to say, "Let me help you." But I didn't.

As I left, I heard her say, "Sometimes, Lord, I don't understand you at all. And, to be honest, I don't like it."

I MET JORN AT the Strawberry B&B. Guests nodded to us from porch rockers as we mounted the steps, and proprietress Ellen Lacey, in her usual high heels, smiled as she rose on her toes and watered the hanging baskets overflowing with purple verbena and petunias as red as her nail polish and shoes. "Go on in," Ellen said. "They're waiting for you in the parlor. There's tea *and* coffee." Ellen winked at Jorn.

"A woman after my own heart." Jorn placed a hand on his chest.

Ellen laughed, waved us into the house, and returned to her watering.

As we entered the quiet foyer, I whispered, "You keep drinking that stuff and you'll pay." Too much caffeine causes muscle tightness, as I liked to remind Jorn when he was groaning in yoga class.

"Stop spoiling my fun," he whispered back.

We found René waiting for us in Ellen's large, welcoming parlor, and I was surprised to see Marie-Jacques Dubois with him. I had expected René, who had contacted Jorn and said he was going to be in the Twin Cities on a buying trip. There had been no mention that his mother was accompanying him. They were seated on a comfortable sofa, heads together in conversation, a silver tea service, pot of coffee, and basket of croissants on the low table in front of them.

After an exchange of handshakes and air kisses, Jorn and I sat in easy chairs opposite the sofa. Madame Dubois poured coffee for Jorn and tea for me. Jorn and I each reached for warm croissants that shattered in freshness down our shirt fronts with the first bite.

"Ellen is known for her croissants," I told Madame Dubois.

She nodded. "We've been impressed with our care here," she said. "Mademoiselle Lacey must have some French in her."

I knew Ellen came from solid British stock, but said, "Perhaps." Turning to René, I asked, "Has your shopping trip been successful?"

René straightened his trendy narrow tie and leaned forward. "I have been quite pleased with my efforts so far."

"And you don't mind being housed so far from the Cities?" Jorn asked, taking a sip of coffee.

"It is good for one to see the countryside," René said. "And it is most convenient for *Maman*."

"Really?" I watched the Frenchwoman finger the large jeweled cross on the gold chain at her neck. Her chin-length silver hair was swept stylishly from her face, a face that was both serene and regal. Even on a summer morning, when all the other visitors on the front porch were dressed in T-shirts and sandals, Madame Dubois wore a tasteful floral suit dress.

"*Maman* is attending the tent revival nearby. So, how do you say it, we killed two birds with one stone," René laughed.

Somehow, I couldn't imagine the elegant Madame Dubois wandering among the crowds, munching on mini-donuts, and waiting for rapture in a sweltering, mosquito-plagued tent. Rapture would come to her in a cool room with high ceilings in an elegant French chateau, and it would come on her schedule—after she finished her tea and croissant. I turned to Madame Dubois and found her attention on Jorn. For just a moment, her pale blue eyes grew hard then she blinked and I wondered what I had seen, what energy had swept through the room.

"Madame Dubois," I said, "I thought you were Catholic." She slowly focused on me. "*Oui.*"

"I wouldn't think a tent revival in a small town like ours would be your style."

"I was raised Catholic, and I raised René and Gasquet in the church." Again her hand went to the beautiful cross, and the blue eyes now bore into me. "But we never know where faith will call us."

A hush fell in the convivial room. It was as if a shadow had passed over the book-lined walls, the game boards and puzzles set up on the tables. René cleared his throat. "We also are anxious to hear of your progress regarding Gasquet."

Jorn and I exchanged a look. Madame Dubois noticed, put down her teacup, and leaned closer. "What is it? What have you found?"

It was Jorn's decision how much to tell the Duboises. I waited. He ruffled his already messy hair and gave them a hapless shrug. "I don't know what to make of it."

"What is it, Peter?" Madame Dubois's tone softened, a mother's concern.

"I think I have heard from Gasquet."

"You think?" René's brow wrinkled in confusion.

"I've received text messages from Gasquet's phone."

Madame Dubois gasped and lifted fingertips to her lips. "From my son?"

Jorn held up his hand in warning. "They're from his phone. That doesn't necessarily mean they're from Gasquet."

"But who else could they be from?" René asked, leaning forward.

"Anyone who has Gasquet's phone," I said. They looked at me as if I were speaking alien.

Madame Dubois straightened. "Text him back. Please, Peter, tell him to come home. Now."

Jorn shook his head. "I've tried. He isn't responding to my messages."

"You mean, you don't think he's getting them?" René asked, then after a pause, "Or he doesn't want to answer them?"

When Jorn only shrugged, René's voice changed. "What actually happened on that last assignment, Peter?"

"I told you," Jorn said.

"What are you holding back?" Suspicion flared in René's face.

Jorn didn't like the inference. He put his coffee cup down with a snap.

Madame Dubois quickly intervened. "René!" she squeezed her son's hand in reassurance. "We know Peter has nothing but love for Gasquet. Please, Peter, what did the message say?"

With obvious effort, Jorn tore his stare from René and turned to Gasquet's mother. He spoke gently to Madame Dubois. "It indicated Gasquet was here. In Minnesota."

"Here? Doing what?" a baffled Madame Dubois asked.

"Watching me."

Jorn did not explain the nature of Gasquet's communications. Was he shielding the truth from Gasquet's mother, that something had become twisted in her son? Or was he hiding the truth from himself—that Gasquet was playing a game and none of us knew the rules?

With a satisfied nod, Madame Dubois rose. We all quickly got up as well. "Then it is good I am here. Please, Peter, I pray you will find my son and bring him to me. If anyone can find Gasquet, I know it is you, his dear friend. If you require my assistance, I will be here all week."

"All week?" I asked.

"Yes, at the revival. I am Sister MJ."

CHAPTER 17

THE DROP OF
A HAND

WE HELD HANDS AS we walked, as we had done for as long as I could remember, in any number of cities and on any number of occasions. I don't know if I reached for hers first or she reached for mine. When Evie and I traveled together, usually to see an art exhibit that Larry didn't have time for and Heart wasn't interested in, we walked everywhere. Once coming out of the Metropolitan Museum in New York, we passed two men sitting on a stone wall, people watching and commenting on everyone they saw. One nodded toward us and said to the other, "That's a mother and daughter." Perhaps it was our similar slender shapes, bent toward each other, eagerly planning our next adventure. Perhaps it was our hats, identical pink baseball caps we bought off a Chinese street vendor that morning with New York spelled "Nu York." Or maybe it was the clasped hands.

On this warm Friday evening, quiet with so many gone to lake cabins and others drawn to the pre-revival excitement at the Chapel of the Forgiving Heart, we circled Lake Michael in Gabriel's Garden and discussed my grandmother. We both wore Capri pants, tanks, and our pink hats; I'd tucked my long hair inside mine in hope of catching the kiss of the evening breeze on my neck. It felt still and muggy at ground level, but rattling high up in the aspens held out hope for a cooler possibility.

"I haven't lifted a paintbrush since she got here," Evie said. From anyone else, this admission would have sounded like a complaint, but my mother never whined. I have always sensed the survivor in my mother. Without knowing all the details, I know she has lived through darkness and come out the other side. This is why I think Evie should have inherited the Down Dog Diary; she is a more fitting keeper than I. She was the one who truly helped people. I'll never understand why Tum gave the diary to me.

"Gran does seem to suck the energy from a place," I said.

Evie didn't argue. "I remember the first time I met Sylvia. I was terrified. Larry insisted I come with him to tell his mother that he was quitting college in California and we were moving to New Mexico. He had already bought the land with some of his trust fund money."

"The land for Whispering Spirit Farm?"

"Yes. Sylvia lived in Seattle. We flew there from Los

Angeles, my first airplane ride. I flew like an innocent dove into the hawk's nest." I could see my grandmother as a hawk, circling until just the right moment when she would swoop down on an unprotected future daughter-in-law.

"The house was more than I had ever imagined." Evie's voice softened with memory. "There was more of everything: food, rooms, Aubusson rugs, chandeliers, forks, rules, servants. Servants. Can you imagine?"

It must have been intimidating, for a dove. My mother had been raised on a farm in Missouri, low country, a land susceptible to the flooding of the Mississippi every few years. As a child, she had stepped back from the waters rising to her porch and seen coffins covered in snakes float by. That, she said, was why she liked Whispering Spirit Farm, sitting so high on a dry New Mexico mountain. Larry had bought the land with her in mind.

"I had no concept of Sylvia's world, no road map, and, to make matters worse, I was an older woman," she drew the last words out and wiggled her eyebrows at me. I laughed.

"How old were you then?"

"I was twenty-one, and Larry was twenty."

"A woman of experience," I teased.

"Obviously, I would lead him down the road to perdition, her poor young son who was getting nothing out of college but a good buzz every night in the fraternity."

"Larry, in a fraternity? You're kidding." The vision of conformity wouldn't come.

Evie gave a little shudder. "He was awful before I got a hold of him. Smart but spoiled. Sylvia had his whole life planned out for him—a prestigious college, a fraternity where he could make the most useful connections, and then the law like his father."

I sputtered with disbelief. "Larry would have made a terrible lawyer."

Evie didn't deny it. Larry talked to machines, not people, and he hated systems created to tell him what he could not do. Larry lived in constant quiet rebellion—dodging his domineering mother, crafting game worlds that made him happy, hacking places where he was not meant to be.

"He seems so different around her," I said thoughtfully.

Evie nodded. "I'll never forget that first visit, walking up to those massive doors. There were heavy lion-head knockers like in a castle. I turned to tease Larry about them and . . . saw my happy, spirited Larry just shut down. Right before my eyes."

"It scared you."

"Yes." We continued to walk. The path veered closer to the lake shore, and a mother wood duck led her brood away from us, little bundles of feathers scurrying after her, squeaking, dancing atop the water. That's what mothers do—lead their children from danger. Grandmother Sylvia would have put on the pressure to break up Evie and her son, and amazingly, even as young as they were and as unaccustomed to rebellion as Larry had been at the time, they stood their ground.

Evie's voice took on a secretive tone. "Here's the thing about your father. He fears that even after all these years, she has the power to drag him back to that life."

"Drag him back?"

"To where money is everything, your position, your worth. To be used as carrot or stick."

"But you don't care about money. And neither does Larry."

"Not for himself. He's over that. But he could be lured back to the family coffers, and all the strings attached, if you or I or Heart needed something beyond our considerable means." Evie's eyes grew serious. "He would go back to being Sylvia's boy—for us."

So Larry's line of defense—and Evie's too—was distance, just like the mother wood duck's. I could understand that, but it had kept me from knowing my grandmother, and that filled me with sadness. "But why didn't I know about her?"

Something in my tone had Evie pulling me to a stop, turning toward me, and squeezing my hand. "Oh, Maya, how do I explain it? We never meant to hurt you. In the beginning, we were so young, and Sylvia was so relentless. Your father was used to having everything, and I was used to having nothing. So we believed we had to make a total break from Sylvia and temptation. We hid on a mountaintop with no plumbing, no phone. That's how scared we were. We just had each other and a tent."

Glorious black-eyed Susans and other wildflowers lined the path, and Evie bent, running her finger along the petal of one flower. Without looking up, she said, "We cut her from our life and built a new one at Whispering Spirit. A simple life, a beautiful one. Your father found his confidence there, and he bloomed." Evie's face broke into a happy smile at the memory. "But he couldn't escape his heritage. He has his father's business savvy, and before we knew it, he was making more money than we knew what to do with. After a few years, I think, he felt strong enough to reestablish contact with Sylvia but only from a distance. We wanted to protect you girls from that life."

"Heart knew about her. Why not me?"

Evie straightened and turned toward me. "You were in India when Heart met Sylvia for the first time. Your sister didn't seem interested in pursuing a relationship with Sylvia. Actually, I think Heart didn't want to risk hurting Larry and me."

"You mean, she took your side."

Evie flung her arms up in frustration. "That's the point. We never meant for there to be sides, Maya. It just happened."

"What about Heart's wedding? Was Gran invited to that?" I couldn't imagine my family being so rude as to not invite Larry's mother to such an important event.

"Your grandmother was recovering from a broken hip and couldn't come. She sent an obscenely huge check and a tea set."

I gasped. "She was the one who sent the Tiffany tea set?"

The wedding was held in Gabriel's Garden, and practically the whole town—knowing either us or hometown boy David—was invited. The tea set overshadowed all the other gifts on the gift table at the reception and was the talk of the event. Made during the Aesthetic Movement, somewhere between 1870 and 1890, it was crafted of numerous metals including copper, platinum, and Japanese gold and was decorated with dragonflies and butterflies. The set, which Heart never uses or even allows Sadie to touch, includes a teapot, coffee pot, creamer, sugar bowl, hot milk jug, kettle, and tray. Probably one of the most expensive tea sets in the world, it was unusual and over-the-top as wedding gifts go in Gabriel's Garden.

"Sylvia," Evie paused, searching for the words, "fills a space, even when she isn't there. I hate how Larry changes in her presence, gets quiet and moody. So it was easier to just stop talking about her. Sylvia simply dropped off our radar and out of our vernacular."

"That still doesn't explain—"

Evie sighed, and when she looked at me, there was guilt in her eyes. "Maybe we never welcomed your grandmother because we knew you would pull her back into our lives."

"I don't understand."

"You're strong like she is. You would fight for her, Maya, and we were afraid."

Guru Bob once told me, "Fear is the strongest emotion. It is behind the ugly words, the fist, the gun, the inexplicable action. Recognize the fear."

Guru Bob was a lot more enlightened than I was. So he probably would have no trouble accepting his parents' "inexplicable" deletion of a grandmother from his life. I was not so cool with the idea. Still, in some way, I understood it. Larry and Evie hated confrontation. They had built an entire community—Whispering Spirit Farm—on that premise. They didn't want to fight with Grandmother or me.

Evie knew me too well. Had I known about Gran Sylvia, I would have wanted to fix the rift between her and my parents. It would have been easy for me, free of the personal baggage of family history, to want to pull my crusty grandmother into the loving arms of family. In my naiveté and need to help the people I love, I would have blundered in. Maybe that would have been a good thing. Maybe not.

After several moments, we started down the lake path again. Gabriel's Garden had not seen rain for weeks, and our footsteps echoed on the packed earth. "There are no pictures of her around the house," I said.

"She refuses to be photographed."

"You mean like the camera will steal her spirit?"

Evie laughed. "No, she's just vain."

I pondered this. Grandmother was not a beautiful woman, and she knew it. She had long ago decided being neat and dignified would have to do. No, it wasn't vanity. "Photos must make her feel out of control," I said. "You never know how they're going to come out."

"I never thought about it like that, but you're probably right."

"Have you ever painted her?"

"Yes, once."

I tried to imagine the painting, and the very thought made me uneasy. Evie's portraits were not sweet—she painted what she saw inside people. Grandmother likely had come out as a grumpy toad: big lips, long warty fingers clutching her handbag, an ill-fitting spring suit and mud-splattered pillbox hat, a superior lift of one wild, hairy brow. Or Evie could just as easily have depicted her as road kill.

"What did you do with it?"

Evie let out a long, cleansing breath. "I painted over it. I didn't want that thing in my house."

Road kill it was.

I looked out over the calm lake, where the reflection of

the trees dived into the water like another forest. "She's still mad that you took Larry away from her."

"How do you know—" Evie shook her head. "Well, she never would have held him. He was already flying away when I met him."

"Still, she blames you."

Evie laughed, lifting her cheek to the breeze. "I sound so evil."

"Maybe Larry had to go through the fires of Sylvia to find you. Like a quest." I could tell from Evie's expression that she liked the romance of that thought.

The woman who claimed she knew my father long before they met, lifetimes ago, in fact, said, "Don't we all have a quest in our hearts?"

As for quests, my current one to find Gasquet and end this cat-and-mouse game was not going well. Just two evenings ago, Jorn's neighbor had chased off a man trying to pry open a window in Jorn's kitchen. Randy had come screaming out of his house, a skinny scarecrow banging a spoon against the hub cap on which he kept Jorn's spare key. He surprised the intruder, who vaulted the back fence and ran away. When Jorn and I arrived, Randy was still shaking. As Jorn examined the slit cut in the screen of the kitchen window, I told Randy that he'd been exceptionally brave but suggested maybe next time he should call the police first.

"Man, all I could think of was make noise," Randy said. "I mean, I don't own a gun. No way, those things are dangerous. And I know like zero kung fu. But I know how to make noise. Peter, you think Armadillo is okay? This was a lot of drama, man, like inches away from her."

Randy had been too busy sending up a clatter, waking up all the dogs in the neighborhood, and saving Armadillo the cactus to notice much about the man. He offered Officer Holmes an unhelpful description of dark clothes, medium build, and masked face. The officer and I were nearly on a first-name basis; he had investigated a burglary at my house a few months ago. Scribbling in his small, official-looking notebook, he said, "You people sure live interesting lives."

When I told Evie about the saving of Armadillo, she stopped at an empty bench, took my hand again, and pulled me down beside her. "Do you think the burglar was looking for the Mourner?"

"What else?" I shrugged.

"I hope it doesn't bring you trouble," said Evie, leaning close, her shoulder against mine.

The alabaster figure of a grieving choirboy had been bundled in a soft old Pendleton scarf belonging to Jorn's uncle and placed in the safe beside the Down Dog Diary, which was swaddled once again in my lovely paisley pashmina.

"Larry assures me my hidden safe is impregnable."

Evie said, "Your father knows—"

I felt an insect buzz my ear and turned to say something to Evie. But she had dropped my hand, broken our connection. As I reached for her, I saw a red flower bloom, like tie dye, on her pink cap.

CHAPTER 18

KARMA KILLER

I ONLY REMEMBER SOME OF the sounds of that night: the EMTs' shoes slapping the hard path and equipment banging against their knees, keys jingling, Larry calling Evie's name over and over, Heart telling me to "Let go now," crows screaming.

So many sounds, but I never heard the gunshot.

Apparently, I had speed dialed everyone on the planet: 9-1-1, Larry, Heart, Jorn, probably even Spirit. The paramedics raced Evie to Saint Paul, where she was hustled into surgery. Brain surgery. As a stranger tunneled through Evie's skull to retrieve a bullet, repair the damage it had done, and keep her alive, we huddled in the lounge in stunned silence. We watched the hands on the clock creep by and prayed to whomever we trusted would hear us. I couldn't stop rubbing my hands. Although I'd washed them, they still felt as if they were covered in Evie's blood.

SATURDAY SLIPPED AWAY FROM us in agonizingly slow moments as we all began to adjust to a new kind of life: waiting for Evie to wake up. It was Sunday morning. Already I hated the waiting and this room of waiting where the windows didn't open, where I couldn't breathe without being filled with the energies of others. The bombardment of despair and hope, anger and grief, was almost unbearable. My only refuge was my chanting and my yoga practice.

Through the chants in my head came the call of the bells of the one-hundred-year-old Cathedral of Saint Paul on Summit Hill. I could see its distinctive copper dome and light gray granite walls from the lounge window. On high, it sent the message out to the city below: *Come. Get right with God.* I imagined that sentiment was an easy one to sell in this room. I pulled into myself, my hands forming fists as the energies of the hospital closed in around me. From the edge of my vision, a hand reached in and gently uncurled the fingers of one hand.

Jorn.

He pulled me into his arms and kissed the top of my head. We were all alone in this vast waiting room down the hall from the intensive care unit where Evie slept. Refusing to leave Evie's side, Larry was parked in a chair by her bed. Heart, keeping calm by keeping busy, had driven Grandmother back to Gabriel's Garden. Gran was upset, silent, watchful of her son but not knowing how to help him.

148

When Heart groaned and said, "I've had enough of these chairs. Let me take you home, Grandmother," Gran hadn't argued. She was clearly exhausted. She'd been at the hospital all night and day with the rest of us. Gran allowed us to help her to her feet. David would babysit Grandmother, and Heart would return later, with food no doubt. Before leaving, Grandmother paused in front of me and gave me a look that I understood—she was leaving the care of her son to me, for now, and Spirit help me if I failed her.

Jorn didn't talk. He just held. And the constriction in my chest grew tighter and tighter until a sob squeezed out. That was all it took to open the gates and flood Jorn. Still, he held on. He felt so solid, just what I needed when my world was unraveling. When the heaviness of heart gave way to emptiness, I whispered a weary sigh, wiped my eyes, and dropped my head to his shoulder. We sat that way for a long time.

Finally, I swore softly, "I'm going to find that fucker, whoever it is."

"Already on it," Jorn said.

I lifted my head and looked at him. "Then you, too, think the bullet was intended for me."

He frowned. "On what planet would someone be after Evie? You, on the other hand . . ."

"Yeah." The guilt came back swinging sledgehammers.

Jorn pulled his small Moleskine notebook from his back pocket. "I've already started a list of people you've pissed off lately."

The bells of the cathedral tolled again. *Come. Get right with God.* All night, my head had buzzed with one thought, circling, stinging: Evie was hurt, maybe even dying, because of me.

"What if it's all my fault?" I whispered.

"What?"

"It should be me lying in that hospital bed with a hole in my head."

"Nonsense," Jorn said, but after seeing the look in my eyes, his expression changed. He leaned closer and lowered his voice, "Maya, is there something I should know?"

I ran my hands up and down my thighs. A chant rose in my head automatically, a chant from long ago, the one I'd repeated over and over as I flew across the Atlantic, fleeing from what I'd done in a city alley. The chant for forgiveness.

With a gesture, Jorn calmed my hands. "You don't have to tell me. Just—is this something that's going to come back to bite us?"

Just like that he was circling the wagons, preparing to protect me. Us, he'd said. I liked that, the idea of us, even though I didn't deserve it.

"Don't you see? It already has."

Jorn frowned. "What are you talking about?"

I rubbed my arms, so cold in the air-conditioned room. "An eye for an eye."

"Maya—"

"I took a life." The words rushed from my mouth. There, I'd said it; now he knew. I waited for a reaction, but Jorn had donned his nonjudgmental reporter's face.

"I set this in motion," I said, abruptly standing and beginning to pace. "Maybe the Universe is looking for a life in trade for the one I took."

That was one explanation the reporter could not accept.

Jorn jumped to his feet and grabbed me by the arms. "Stop it. I don't believe in that shit."

"Karma," I said, holding his stare.

"I don't believe in karma either," he said. "Now, sit down, and we'll figure this out."

He tugged at my arm until, finally, I turned and sat back down in the hard waiting-room chair. After several moments, I whispered, "I don't even know his name."

"Who?"

"The man I killed."

Jorn didn't rush me. He sat down beside me, close, and waited.

"I was in New York," I began. "It was dark, and I was walking down the street. Then I heard a sound, the sound of someone getting the shit beaten out of them. I heard a woman cry out, and I couldn't just keep walking."

"Of course, you couldn't."

"He was so big, and she was so small, curled up in the trash. I could smell her fear." The hand on top of mine turned, and we were holding hands. "It was raining. Street smells coming out with the rain, rotting food, wet boxes. And yet, I smelled her fear."

I paused, and I heard it again in my mind, the grunt as she took a kick in the ribs. That's when everything faded away—the car horns, a siren somewhere, the laughter of people on the street, the smells. I found myself in that quiet place of total focus, and I began to run down the alley.

"He was going to kill her," I said, my eyes seeking Jorn's, seeking some understanding. "I just wanted to push him away."

"I know."

"But then—"

"He hit you."

I heard the man's voice again, "Get the fuck outta here. This ain't your business."

That had never stopped me before. On the ground, my cheek hurting like hell, I was level with the woman. Our eyes met. Her face was a mix of blood, tears, smeared makeup, and resignation. That was what really hurt. She had been here before, probably with this very man, and she had no hope anything would change. The man turned his back on me and started in on the woman again. "When I send your ass out on the street, I expect full return. Fucking junkie whore."

He pulled his leg back to give her another kick, and she curled tighter, trying to protect herself. I pulled myself up and punched him in the kidney.

"Yeah," I said to Jorn. "He hit me, but I wasn't like the woman he was kicking like a dog. I hit back. That made him mad. He came at me. I defended myself, dodging and parrying, until I saw my chance."

"Your chance?"

"I put everything into one kick to the throat. One mother of a kick. One lucky kick."

Jorn squeezed my hand.

I had begun to rock. I was back in that alley. "Tum always said anything can happen in a fight," I whispered.

Jorn waited.

"There was a piece of rebar sticking out of the wall. He flew back into it. Hit it just right. Because he just stuck there. Like a butterfly on a pin."

The man looked at me that last time, astonished. He

couldn't have been more incredulous than I was. As I saw the light leave his eyes, I bent over, grabbing my belly. What had I done?

Behind me, the woman gasped. I turned toward her, holding out a hand, but she didn't take it. With huge eyes, the woman looked from the man to me. Without a word, she scrambled out of the trash and stumbled out of the alley.

"I never intended for him to die," I said softly. Silently, I begged for forgiveness—from Spirit, from Jorn, from the man in the alley.

Jorn's hand was warm, wrapped around mine. He sighed. "Shit happens."

His calm acceptance reminded me of Tum. I closed my eyes and heard Tum's gravelly voice on the day he tracked me down at the ashram in India, "Some things can't be changed, kid. They aren't meant to be. They're karma killers, and that's the bitch of life."

I opened my eyes and faced Jorn. "I killed my karma that night, Jorn. And this is my punishment."

I saw Jorn pull himself back and pretend that he was not affected by my confession. "I don't believe that. You saved a life. Period." Watching me from the corner of his eye, he flipped open his notebook, taking us back to business. This tough love approach was so like Tum and Guru Bob that I nearly laughed. So that was that; discussion closed.

Jorn looked at his notes. "I've talked to the police. The bullet is from a .9mm semi-automatic handgun. It's fairly common. With Minnesota's conceal-and-carry law, it could be hidden in a holster on the hip under any asshole's shirt."

"That's comforting."

"The police believe the shooter was fairly close, within fifteen feet. They found spent shells in the woods. Do you remember seeing anyone around the lake?"

I thought back to that evening. I remember the wood duck protecting her brood and the aspen leaves sparkling as the setting sun flickered in the tops of the trees. I remember Evie unrolling soft memories with a smile. We'd had the place to ourselves, or so I had thought. There was quiet and then—I shook my head; I had seen no one.

"Have you ever shot a handgun?" I asked.

Jorn said, "Yes. Loud with a kick."

"Has Gasquet ever shot a handgun?"

Jorn froze. "Don't go there."

"We know he's here. And he's pissed. Maybe he wants the Mourner back, maybe he wants revenge for you leaving him on that mountain."

"I didn't leave him!"

"You weren't there when he woke up. You were gone."

Jorn shook his head. "No, no."

"Jorn, you and I know you would have stayed with Gasquet, if you could have. But *he* doesn't know that. In his eyes, you left him."

"Why would he shoot you?"

That question had been tumbling around in the back of my mind. I'd never even met Gasquet. My only connection to him was through Jorn. "To get to you."

"I can't believe it. I won't believe it." Jorn stood, shoved his hands in his pockets, and walked over to the window. He stared out at the cathedral on the hill. It's hard beauty reminded me of Gasquet's alabaster Mourner, for that is how

I had come to think of the sculpture sitting in my safe. Even if it was one of the tomb sculptures from the Court of Burgundy, to me, it was grieving Gasquet, not some egotistical old duke.

I joined Jorn at the window and knuckled my eyes. It had been a long time since I had slept, truly slept, not napped curled like a pretzel in a waiting-room chair.

"Okay," I said in a calming voice. "Who else do we have?"

Jorn took a moment, then gathered his thoughts. "There's our trigger-happy PTSD nutcase, Val."

"After what we saw the other night," I said, "Val is a definite possibility. But if he did this—Tessa or no Tessa—he's going down."

Jorn nodded. "I'll check him out."

"Be careful," I said.

"I'm covering the tent revival for *The Independent*. While I'm there, I'll have a chat with Val."

I nodded. "And there's the guy who tried to break into your house. He's an X-factor."

"He's a burglar, not a murderer. Besides, if he were going to knock off anyone, it would be Randy and his damn clanging hubcap."

I grinned at Jorn. "Randy's just trying to be responsible. He doesn't want to lose your key."

"So he uses a hubcap?" Jorn rubbed his forehead as if the very thought of his stoner neighbor gave him a headache.

We stood together at the window for a long time, watching Saint Paul wake up and swing itself into its Sunday routine. Both of our minds were tired, and movement seemed beyond us.

Without turning to me, Jorn said, "Do you want me to check on Bella?"

My cat was probably lonely and taking it out on the red sofa, but it wasn't necessary for Jorn to babysit her. "She's good," I said. Her feeder operated on a timer, and she had enough food to last for days.

"I still might drop by," he said. Lately, Bella had grown more adventurous in yoga class. Instead of just watching from under the Buddha table, she had begun wandering carefully between the mats and invariably she stopped to rub against Jorn's leg when he was in Down Dog. Jorn pretended not to like it.

"You know where the key is?"

"Under the cairn of rocks by the door." He turned then, walked over to the chairs where we had been sitting, and picked up a long object. It was a yoga mat. He handed it to me. "I thought you might want this. To help you wait." It was not one of the brightly colored mats I kept in the studio for drop-ins. Both the mat and its carrying bag were new and black.

"You bought a mat?" I said in surprise. Jorn had always insisted he wouldn't be taking yoga long enough to warrant the expense. He usually borrowed from the studio.

"It's a man's mat," Jorn said. "No flowers or girly colors."

I hid a smile. "I see."

"And don't get it all sweaty. I'll want it back."

After Jorn left, I unrolled the mat in a corner of the lounge and sat in lotus pose, pulling in the silence of the room. Soon it would start filling up with visitors, but for now I had the room to myself. There, on Jorn's thick mat, I felt comforted; it was a piece of home.

I opened my satchel and pulled out the Down Dog Diary that I had taken from the safe before rushing to the hospital. I opened the book to a random page and inhaled the scent of bubblegum. The handwriting was that of James Tumblethorne. I read:

I knew I had to leave the gang when the fighting began to make me sick. I can tell you exactly the day it happened: the name of the bar and the town and the face I'd just rearranged. I rode into the desert so the others wouldn't see me puke. I can still taste the regret, and regret wasn't supposed to be part of our lives.

We seek to hurt what hurts us, Spirit. Crazy, huh? Don't we know that we are they?

CHAPTER 19

CONFESSIONS
IN THE DARK

B Y MONDAY AFTERNOON, THE hospital room had become dishearteningly familiar. Our home away from home. It was where Evie was, and for Larry, Heart, and me, there was no other place. We'd been told that, at times, those in comas can and do hear the people talking to them and even respond. So we weren't taking any chances. Someone had to be there at all times, just in case Evie heard one of us and opened her eyes, just in case she shrugged off the machines and breathing tubes, just in case a miracle happened.

The neurosurgeon could not tell us how much damage had been done to Evie's brain. Would she talk again and walk and eat her favorite cereal? Would she paint again? Would she remember us?

"We've induced a coma to protect the brain and give it time to heal," the neurosurgeon told us.

Still, we all would have been happier if she would start breathing on her own. The sound of the ventilator helping her was incessant, and by now part of the new normal, as were the footsteps of the kind but noncommittal nurses and the rattle of carts outside the door and the whispers of other families drifting past on the way to other rooms full of more machines and people struggling to break free of them.

I stood by the window, where a crow had been keeping vigil on the ledge outside. I listened to Larry talk to Evie, as usual her hand clasped in his. Hearing was the last sense to go, the nurses told us, and so we dared not let go of that slender rope. Evie had to know that we were there, ready to pull her from whatever abyss she had fallen into. We whispered stupid things: "Your hospital gown is an ugly green with pink trim." We resurrected memories: "Remember when Maya broke her arm? She must've been about three. You grabbed her up, bundled her in a sling across your chest, and climbed on the back of Tum's motorcycle. You hated that motorcycle, but the van and truck weren't there. Tum flew down that mountain, nearly wiping out on the hairpin turns, so desperate were you both to get to a hospital. I know you were scared shitless, but—"

When Larry's voice broke, I quickly sat down in another chair beside the bed and took hold of my mother's other hand. For three days now, I had held this frail appendage and prayed to Spirit for help, to give a small sign, a weak but reassuring squeeze. Nothing. I put on a cheerful but stern voice, "Okay, Evie, it's time to wake up. Because Heart's driving us all nuts." That's what we did when the moment got too heavy to lift: one of us would shift gears. We were a relay team, carrying the baton forward when one of us tired. I saw Larry's lips soften into the beginnings of a smile and went on. "You know how Heart gets when she's stressed. She's cooking and cleaning and fussing. You've got to wake up, Evie, and save us."

We each coped with this family emergency in different ways. For Heart, it was cooking. Every day she appeared cooler in hand. We were being buried alive by packets of mystery food carefully wrapped in aluminum foil or sealed in one of Heart's numerous plastic containers.

For Larry, it was research. He handled things best when he was given a mission. When he wasn't talking to Evie, he was planted in the lounge, tapping on his laptop, trolling the Internet for articles and papers on "brain injuries," and calling and emailing doctors all over the world. Even though Evie was receiving the best of care in this hospital in Saint Paul, Larry had to *do* something. He was probably driving the doctors here mad; every time he saw them he had more questions and theories and "what do you think about so-and-so's work in . . ." The doctors were amazingly patient with him. They knew he was afraid, as was everyone in this unit.

As I was. I dealt with this huge monkey wrench by hitting the yoga mat, meditating, filling my head with chants, and taking care of Evie's mail.

Word had spread fast of Evie's shooting. Letters and

get-well cards from neighbors in Gabriel's Garden and emails from friends around the world, including Whispering Spirit Farm, had begun flooding in to Larry. So many offers of help, so many prayers and healing energies sent. Heart had taken over answering the emails, while Larry did his research. I opened the cards and letters and read them all, every word, to Evie.

I slit the edge of an elegant envelope and pulled out a card of heavy-weight ivory stationery, folded in half. The black ink was from a fountain pen, the flowing letters pressing into the fibers of the paper. The handwriting was strong and beautiful. I read:

Do not lose faith.
God is near, holding your hand.
I will keep you in my prayers.
Marie-Jacques Dubois

I must admit I was surprised that Madame Dubois had taken the time to dash off this note and so quickly after the accident. She didn't know Evie or Larry.

I leaned toward Evie and teased her, "Well, you've got Madame Dubois praying for you. That's got to open some doors. She's the great and powerful Sister MJ, you know." As soon as I said the words, the pain of possibly losing Evie lanced through me. Evie thought *everyone* was great and powerful. That was Evie's secret weapon. My mother was like no one I had ever met; Sister MJ couldn't even compare.

Evening crept down the streets and slid into the hallways and rooms. The hospital began to quiet. Tired visitors shuffled home where hungry families waited, where life went on as normal. Heart had left hours ago to drive back to Gabriel's Garden to care for Sadie, while David took Grandmother to tonight's revival meeting. Laughing when she calls him the gardener, David gets along with Grandmother better than Heart, who takes umbrage at much of what Grandmother says. I think David has figured out the old bird, sees past the rudeness to a pocket of fear, a vulnerability I saw as well. My grandmother was afraid of not being able to reach her son when he most needed her.

I stroked Evie's soft hand. Every day, I massaged her arms and hands with lotion, not because the skin was dry but because I knew she would like it. I'd brought a bottle from her immense collection of lotions, something with a strong scent—gardenia—to battle the stale, antiseptic smells of the hospital.

Larry and I were talked out. We sat next to Evie letting our energies do the talking. My body ached. In a few minutes, I would go to the lounge, which would be nearly empty by now, and unroll Jorn's yoga mat in one quiet corner. That had become my evening ritual. I moved from one asana to another, tears dripping on the mat, and then I sat in lotus and quietly chanted. Chant, chant, chant until the urge to sob went away, until my heart didn't flutter as I breathed, until the world seemed bearable again.

I looked with love on my father's bent head, his graying hair slipping out of his ponytail. His long arms were draped over his knees. He wore a flannel shirt against the chill of the hospital room. I tucked Evie's blanket more securely under her chin. As he studied his black high-top tennis shoes, he began to talk, "We've always found each other, you know?"

"I know." My parents believed their souls have always been entwined and always would be.

"We are meant to be together. She cannot leave like this. It's not right."

"She's not leaving us," I reassured him.

It was at times like these, when things slowed in the intensive care unit, when he and I were alone, that memories bubbled to the surface and brought some peace to Larry. He couldn't help himself; he had to talk about her. "We met in front of Grauman's Chinese Theatre in Hollywood," Larry sat back with a sigh. "What a place. What a girl. Your mother was looking at Sophia Loren, and I was looking at her."

"Sophia Loren?"

"She was staring at Sophia Loren's handprint in the courtyard. But none of those stars could compare to your mother. I couldn't take my eyes off her. She glowed, man, like a golden light on a dark night. I had to talk to her."

I knew the story, or most of it. "She told you to go away. Get lost, you ridiculous man."

He nodded. "She was prettier, but I was smarter. I knew she was the one. I followed her like a puppy to that dump where she worked. Sat in that booth for hours just waiting for her to notice me."

"She should have called the cops on you."

"Your mother would never do that."

"You were a rich college kid, spoiled, and couldn't understand why a waitress barely making it on tips wouldn't just fling her apron aside and fly away with you."

"I was an idiot. I didn't deserve her, still don't. I lived on an allowance and complained. She lived hand to mouth and didn't care. She blew me away. Then, for some reason, I will never understand, she decided to save me."

I leaned forward. This was new territory. "How?"

Larry gathered his thoughts. "You may not know this, but Evie has been on her own since she was fifteen."

"That long?"

"Her mother died when she was young, leaving her with a father who worked hard and drank harder. He was a laborer on a farm. Liked to hunt and fish. He left her alone a lot. He didn't know what to do with a girl growing into a beautiful woman, didn't know how to protect her."

I glanced at my mother's pale, still face, her head wrapped in a white bandage. I couldn't see her hair, and that bothered me; it made her seem vulnerable and not like the strong mother I thought I knew. And now Larry was speaking of a vulnerable young Evie. "What happened?" I whispered, not knowing if I wanted to hear this.

"It was an accident," Larry said, a note of defense in his voice. "Evie and her dad lived in a cabin on the Mississippi. I've been there, a desolate place, no neighbors. At night, you can hear voices carrying over the water. They come out of the fog and creep into your soul." Larry paused, cleared his throat. "It was no place for a girl alone. Her father was off drinking most nights, and boys had begun coming up to the house at night, crashing through the woods on their ATVs, making noises. Scaring her. Some nights, she was so terrified—"

"Oh no."

Larry's eyes found mine. "She'd begun sleeping with one of her father's guns."

I couldn't believe it. "But she hates guns."

"With a passion." His expression was thoughtful, sad, and a bit angry. "One night, she heard someone rattling the door, trying to get in. She yelled, 'Go away,' but they kept trying to get in." He paused. "She fired two shots through the door."

I gasped. "The boys?"

Larry shook his head. "Her father, drunk, unable to get the door unlocked."

My eyes closed in pain for a moment then I looked at him. "Was he . . .?"

Larry held my gaze. "No, he survived, but Evie didn't know that. She was a scared kid who thought she'd killed her own father. She ran. Hitched a ride to California. Lied about her age to get work."

"Poor Evie."

My heart went out to that young Evie who had to face the world alone. Such a condition was incomprehensible to me who had always had the support of Evie, Larry, and Heart, not to mention Tum and the huge, crazy family of Whispering Spirit.

"She was haunted by guilt and fear. For a long time, she kept to the shadows, jumping at every passing cop car, avoiding connections. She didn't make friends."

"Except for Paulette," I said.

"Yeah, well, Paulette can batter her way through a castle's defenses with a mascara wand."

"She adopted Evie."

"Evie needed adopting. She thought she was a wanted criminal. She was lost. She didn't know her father had lived and even covered for her."

"Really?" I said, thinking I probably would have liked my grandfather.

"Told the sheriff he shot himself cleaning his guns. At least, he tried to protect her there at the end. He died of cancer a few years later."

I had no doubt Larry had ferreted out the information about Evie's father, my grandfather, to set Evie's mind at ease. "So how did Evie save you?"

Larry took Evie's limp hand and brought it to his lips. "She ended the loneliness."

CHAPTER 20

RIDE AT UR
OWN RISK

Cars lined the paved county road and the gravel lane leading to the Chapel of the Forgiving Heart. Grandmother Sylvia and I parked in a field at a nearby farm and took a makeshift shuttle service—aluminum lawn chairs arranged in the back of a rusty pickup truck—to the tent revival. A sign taped to the rear window of the old pickup said: *Ride at Ur Own Risk.* We'd paid ten dollars each for use of this questionable conveyance. Several times I had to grab Gran's chair to keep it from tipping into the lap of a weary-looking older man in a work shirt and dusty boots. Everything in the truck rattled, from axle to lawn chairs, making conversation impossible. This wasn't any way for a woman my grandmother's age to be transported. Yet, my grandmother weathered the bumpy ride with a stately posture, staring straight ahead, leather handbag squarely on her lap.

When the truck stopped, the farmer called, "Everybody out," as his son placed a wooden box on the ground behind the truck and began helping passengers disembark. Our traveling companion stepped off the back with the ease of a lifetime of navigating farm equipment, turned, and, with the assistance of the farmer and son, helped my grandmother out of the truck. I thanked him, stepped down next to Gran, and took in the bustling scene.

It was Tuesday night and Sister MJ's first scheduled appearance at the revival. She was why I was here—that and because someone had to drive Grandmother and I was going bats at the hospital, where the situation had not changed. Evie was still unconscious; the machines were still pumping and beeping; and Larry was still waiting, still searching the Internet for answers, still picking at the food bossy Heart kept pushing on him.

The smell of mini-donuts caught my attention. I purchased a small bag and offered one to Grandmother. She looked at it with suspicion. "Is this a Minnesota thing?" she asked.

"I don't know," I said. "To be true Minnesotan, I think it has to be on a stick."

Grandmother looked puzzled, but I didn't bother explaining about the culinary peculiarities of the Minnesota State Fair.

"Well, maybe just one," she said, taking the sugary treat

as if I were handing her a mouse. She bit into the small donut, leaving particles of cinnamon sugar on her lips and fingers. She licked her lips. To wipe her fingers, she dug out a lacy handkerchief from the handbag dangling on her arm.

The grassy field in front of the Chapel of the Forgiving Heart was cut to a stubble and bisected by the gravel lane to the chapel. On one side was an ocean of makeshift accommodations—tents, campers, RVs—and on the other was a huge, red-striped tent. A banner stretched across its entrance:

COME ALIVE WITH GOD
EVERY NIGHT AT 6:30

We elbowed our way through the crowds toward the tent. The air was filled with expectation, fellowship, and that summer evening feeling of cool release. Children chasing each other, business types still in their office suits, suntattooed farmers, dusty construction workers, women in anything from casual summer pants to their Sunday best, texting teens, young parents with babies in strollers, seniors with walkers—all were here to be saved.

Strings of lights glowed warmly inside the tent, whose walls were rolled up on three sides to accommodate the large crowd. I guided Grandmother around a tent rope and peg and through the entrance. We sat down in two wooden folding chairs about midway down the center aisle. I reached into my bag of donuts and couldn't believe it. Gran had eaten them all. I turned to her, but she unrepentantly looked at me and wiped the corner of her mouth with her handkerchief. I crumbled the empty bag and stuffed it into my pocket.

On the stage was a band—bass guitar, drum set, organ, and fiddle—playing a selection of Gospel favorites. The crowd talked over the music, not paying much attention to the musicians until a small girl with a big voice stepped in front of the band and sent a hush shivering through the tent. The guitarist lowered the microphone stand for the child, but she still had to mount an apple crate to reach the old microphone. Younger than Sadie, with tapping bare feet visible under a white eyelet dress, she had a smile like Shirley Temple's and belted out "Amazing Grace" with the vocal purity of Mahalia Jackson. When she closed her eyes, lifted her astonishing voice to the sky, and disappeared in a world of her making, I was glad, for the first time that evening, that I had come.

Someone took the seat beside me. I glanced over and found Peter Jorn smiling at me. I introduced Jorn to Gran. She gave him the once-over then said over the music, "My husband never liked newspapermen."

Jorn just grinned and leaned toward me. "How's Evie?" he asked. "And how's my mat?"

"Your mat's doing better than Evie," I said.

"Sorry."

There had been no change in Evie's condition. "It's been four days," I told him. "Larry looks like shit. Heart's feeding half the lounge."

Jorn shoved his hands in his pockets and studied the ground. He lowered his voice and nodded toward Gran. "And your grandmother?"

"I don't know," I whispered. "She just sits. In silence.

Sometimes with Larry. Sometimes in the lounge. I think she's praying a lot." I paused.

It was sad. I think Gran wanted to comfort her son, but they didn't have that kind of relationship. I couldn't imagine such distance with someone I loved. Heart and I were raised by huggers, demonstrative people who easily and freely wrapped their arms around anyone and anything. Whispering Spirit Farm was full of them.

I turned to Jorn. "What's new?"

He pulled out his notebook and flipped through the pages.

"No .9mm handguns at Val's."

"Are you sure?"

"None registered to him. No conceal and carry permit."

"Would there necessarily be a record if he did own one?"

Jorn shrugged. "He could always buy one at a gun show. It's called the gun show loophole. Selling person to person. You have to be at least twenty-one to buy a handgun and eighteen to buy a long gun in Minnesota. The seller's supposed to check the buyer's ID and, for handguns, the buyer's permits but—"

"Some people ignore the law."

"Yeah." Jorn touched my arm, trying to reassure me. "Look. He showed me the arsenal in his bedroom. It's extremely organized; he's proud of it. I didn't see any .9mms."

Thinking of Tessa living just down the hall from so many weapons made me both scared and angry.

Jorn jumped and reached into his pocket to pull out a vibrating phone. He pressed a button, read the text message, then passed the phone to me.

It was from Gasquet's father, Aristide: *Important that we talk. Coming to the States.*

While Jorn dialed Aristide's number, I tried to remember what we knew about Aristide Dubois. He owned a successful ad agency in Paris, was originally from Cameroon, and, according to René and his mother, had been at odds with Gasquet for most of his life. How did Aristide know about us? How did he get Jorn's number? It must be two in the morning in Paris. What could be so urgent?

When I looked at Jorn, he shook his head. No answer.

AS THE BAND AND the child songstress launched into "When the Saints Go Marching In," Grandmother tugged at my sleeve. I leaned closer to hear her. "More donuts," she said, above the audience clapping in sync to the music.

"Save my seat," I shouted over the din to my grandmother.

"Do I look like an usher?"

"You want mini-donuts or not?"

With a sigh at the imposition, she reached into her purse and drew out a white summer glove. As I rose, she placed it on my seat. Jorn hid a grin and told me to bring back two bags.

While waiting in line at the mini-donut truck, I scanned the milling crowd and spotted Val leaning against a tree. He was neatly dressed in a white buttoned-down shirt and chinos, no visible firearms. Tessa in a summer dress stood beside him. She smiled at me and bowed her head over hands clasped in prayer. *Namaste.* Val said something to her and frowned. Tessa just laughed at him. Jorn had been right about her. She was strong and crazy enough to bring the spirit of yoga to a holy-rolling revival.

I bought donuts and approached Val and Tessa. Val gave me a suspicious look and demanded, "What are you doing here?"

From the moment Grandmother and I stepped off the truck at the revival, I had kept an eye out for anyone looking like Gasquet. I pulled out my phone and showed the siblings the copy of Jorn's photo of Gasquet. I offered them a mini-donut. "Have you guys seen this man?"

Heads together, they studied the image on the phone. Without looking up, Val plucked a donut from the bag in my hand. "What's he done?" he asked, tensing.

Taking in the way Jorn and Gasquet were posed, arms around each other's shoulders, smiling comrades in dusty desert garb, Tessa said, "Jorn's friend?"

"Yeah, but we think he's kind of lost right now."

Tessa's gaze flew to her brother's face, but he was memorizing the photo. She locked looks with me. "Got it. We'll keep an eye out."

"Don't approach him," I said, offering Val another donut. He took the bag. "Just let me know, okay?"

Tessa returned the phone. "Don't worry. It's going to be a quiet week here." There was a thread of steel in her voice. I wouldn't be surprised if Tessa had locked up Val's guns for the duration of the revival. And I wouldn't be surprised if Tessa showed up in yoga class next week. Her usual calm had an air of authority. The energy between her and her brother had shifted since the night Val shredded the foliage with a shotgun. Maybe she could get some help for her brother; if anyone could, it would be Tessa.

I bought another bag of mini-donuts and rejoined Grandmother and Jorn in the tent. Jorn picked up Grandmother's glove and handed it back to her. She tucked it into her handbag then grabbed one of the bags of donuts.

"Did I miss anything?" I asked.

"Reverend Know Nothing is about to get the show rolling," Gran said, delicately biting into a donut.

The exuberant Reverend Harold Miley came running down the center aisle and jumped onto the stage with the showmanship of a ringmaster. The band soared into "I Still Haven't Found What I'm Looking For" by U2. The Reverend Miley was no Bono, but the audience still rocked along with the preacher, his wavy salt-and-pepper tresses swinging against his chin, his smile glowing with rapture. At the end of the song, Reverend Miley whirled, long coattails flying, and applauded the band. Then he was back beaming at the faces in the crowded tent.

"Are you ready to change your life?" he shouted, arms raised to the heavens.

"Yes!" the audience roared.

"Are you ready to rock with the Lord?"

"Yes!"

"Are you ready to find your way back to His ever-loving arms?"

"Amen!"

"Tonight you will leave this tent a changed man, a changed woman, a changed child. He is with us, all around us, in the person next to you. Turn to your neighbor and say, 'Nice to see you, Lord.'"

Throughout the tent, people were turning, shaking hands, speaking to each other. I turned to Grandmother and she said, "Don't even think about it."

I laughed and instead gave her a hug. It was like clutching a board.

Jorn tapped me on the arm. "Maya, you're scaring your grandmother." Gran did look a bit stunned, so I let her go and turned back to the stage and Reverend Know Nothing.

The Reverend Miley then told a story from the Bible about the prodigal son who, according to the preacher, was lost and then found and they celebrated with pizzas for everyone. Grandmother simply shook her head and mumbled, "The man's an idiot."

There were several "acts" between the Reverend Miley's kickoff and Sister MJ's appearance, including a preacher from Tennessee who spent about thirty minutes healing people. "Bring your aches and pains, both emotional and physical; your diseases and sordid afflictions," he invited. People shuffled toward the stage on limping legs and crutches; some rolled up in wheelchairs. They formed a line before the preacher, heads bowed. He moved from one person to the next, placing his hand on their heads and praying over them. "Out, you demon! Out, you cancer! Out, you disease!" he cried. A contingent of strong men was on hand, always surrounding the one being healed. Some would fall back when the preacher shouted, and the men would lower the "cured" to the grass, where they would twitch and babble in tongues that made no sense. Eventually, the men would help or carry the fallen out of the tent.

I glanced at Grandmother, the woman who carries holy

oil in her purse. Her lips were firmly pressed in a frown. She did not approve. I didn't know what to think. From the moment we stepped off the truck, the energy of the event had puzzled me. It was almost overpowering, electrifying, and yet uncomfortable—far different from what I had experienced in other places where people came to be healed, places such as Saint Joseph's Oratory of Mount Royal in Montreal. Every time I visit St. Joseph's basilica, the hopes and dreams of others wash over me like breaking waves. It is a simple chamber; the only decoration on the walls are thousands of crutches, flung off by the healed, all miracles performed by Saint Brother André Bessette. It is said the most devout Catholics climb the basilica's ninety-nine steps on their knees. This tent revival production paled in comparison to crawling one's way to a miracle, leaving wooden crutches in one's wake.

But I never discounted the energy of believers. Belief could move mountains, heal broken bones, twist minds. It could lift or destroy us all.

WITH EACH SONG, EACH preacher, each performance, the energy in the tent ascended. And then Sister MJ took the stage. The audience surged to its feet, welcoming her with applause, shouts, whistles, raised cell phones snapping photos. Jorn and I exchanged looks. This was not the Madame Dubois we had come to know.

The hair was the same—shining silver fashionably cut to chin length; the clothes were signature Madame Dubois in that they were elegant, but the tone was different. Instead of the luxurious suits and dresses Madame Dubois favored, Sister MJ had selected an unpretentious royal blue shirtwaist dress with a flowing skirt. Around her neck was a Hermès silk scarf and Madame Dubois's large jeweled cross with the single pearl drop. The entire presentation was humble yet classy—an interesting persona.

Sister MJ smiled benevolently at the audience, a relaxed and welcoming smile we had never received from Madame Dubois. Finally, she spread her arms as if to embrace us all and said into the nearly invisible wireless headset mic, "*Mes amis, j'taime, j'taime.* My friends, I love you. I love you." This brought answering shouts of adoration from the crowd, and the air shook with the roar of applause.

Sister MJ continued to smile, a motherly blessing, and had to motion several times for the audience to sit. When I'd gone to Sister MJ's website, I'd found a cyber home dedicated to meeting the needs of followers—with prayer circles, inspirational blog posts, daily prayers delivered by email—but little real information about Sister MJ herself, not even a photo. Her bio page was two sentences long: "Sister MJ has been blessed with visions from the Good Lord since she was a young girl in France. Now, she brings that wisdom and faith to others around the world." Sister MJ avoided the limelight and was selective about her appearances. The website was like the woman I saw on the stage: down-to-earth yet polished.

"I come to you tonight because of a vision," Sister MJ's accented voiced flowed out of the large speakers beside the stage. The tent quieted. "I saw people like you struggling, reaching for a mountain in the distance, a glowing hilltop.

So I began to walk toward it and with each step, a voice whispered, 'There is help for the hurting. There is hope for the hopeless. The lost can be found.' What was this voice? I wondered."

I felt my grandmother lean forward and saw her eyes narrow. Then I studied others in the crowded tent as well as the people standing two and three deep outside the tent. Everyone was mesmerized by Sister MJ. The energy of reverence for the woman on the stage swamped me. While everyone else appeared to find comfort in the words of Sister MJ, I felt a growing unease. I reached for Jorn's hand. He looked at me with surprise.

Leaning toward me, he whispered, "What is it?"

I couldn't speak so I just shook my head. He held my hand more tightly.

"My children, I believe in resurrection," Sister MJ said. "I have seen it in my visions. The Almighty has told me of it. You only have to believe. Have faith. Join me and the pain goes away—"

"Amen!" someone shouted and rose from his seat.

"The sin dissolves—"

"Amen!" cried a woman stepping into the center aisle and raising her arms.

"The way becomes clear."

"Yes! Yes!" More people were rising, lifting their arms and faces.

By the end of the revival, the believers were breathing as one body. The world had changed for some of these people, just as the Reverend Miley had predicted. The impossible was possible. Miracles could happen, real ones—Sister MJ had said so. It was a spirit-rousing, hope-filling, comforting performance. Charismatic Sister MJ left Guru Bob in the dust.

Back in the pickup, being shuttled to our car, I asked Grandmother, "Is she the real deal?"

After a long moment of thought, my grandmother, who I surmised was not easily impressed, said, "Yes."

For some reason, this verification from my grandmother disheartened me.

"But," Gran said with a spark in her eye, "that doesn't make her right."

CHAPTER 21

THE SELFIE
FROM HELL

I N YOGA, WE SEEK to immerse ourselves in the moment, to put down the smartphone and stop recording life for a later date, to experience it now in all its living colors and energies.

Evie always told me, "Sink into life, let it surround you like a water bed." Except, there are some moments into which we never want to sink—quicksand moments. Even though we've heard all the instructions about outwitting quicksand, we still struggle and founder in such times.

We still sink.

And those moments usually hit when we are doing the

most innocuous of things such as being escorted home at the end of an evening.

Having been raised on Whispering Spirit Farm and having had no experience with high school, much less high school dating etiquette, I was often caught off guard by the pleasant and old-fashioned custom of a boy seeing a girl to the door. So when Jorn insisted that he follow Grandmother and me home from the tent revival, I thought it was rather sweet. As I walked Gran to Heart's door, I waved Jorn on, and he started home. He had barely travelled a block when I heard him slam on the brakes with a screech. Automatically putting my body between Gran's and the disturbance, I saw Jorn's Jeep make a U-turn and speed back toward us.

Something was wrong.

I hurried Gran to the door and handed her over to Heart, who was waiting for us. She saw my expression and said, "What is it? Grandmother?"

"She's fine," I reassured my sister.

"Someone tell that hot-rodding reporter that hardworking people are trying to sleep," groused Grandmother.

"I'll take care of it, Gran," I said.

As Heart led Grandmother inside, diverting her attention by asking how the tent revival went, my phone chimed with a message.

Jorn was racing up the sidewalk toward me. "Wait!" he called.

I gave him a strange look, pressed the button to see an incoming text, and gasped.

Gasquet had sent me a selfie.

He was dressed in blue hospital scrubs and cap, a surgical mask hiding his features. I saw just a sliver of bronze skin, a mass of dreadlocks springing from the cap, and in the background was Evie lying in her bed. She looked so helpless, tied down with tubes and drugs in a sleep that would not release her. Under the image were two words: *Next time?*

My knees buckled, and I sat heavily on Heart's porch step. Jorn pulled me into his arms, and I clutched his shirt. "I just got the same message," he whispered. "I'm so sorry."

Heart opened the door and scrambled to my side. "What happened? Is it Evie?"

I just shook my head and passed Heart my phone.

Her forehead wrinkled in puzzlement. "Why is someone taking pictures of Evie? Who is that? And where's Larry?"

I straightened, pushed myself out of Jorn's embrace, and grabbed the phone back. Where *was* Larry?

Jorn pulled me to my feet. "Come on. I'll drive."

"I'm coming with you," Heart said. She ran back into the house, gave David some quick instructions, and snatched her purse from the peg by the door.

On the road to Saint Paul, I brought Heart up-to-date on Gasquet's recent messages.

"But what do you think this wacko wants, and why is he in Evie's room?"

"He's not a wacko," Jorn said, but with less conviction than he would have voiced weeks ago.

"What does he want?" Heart asked again.

Jorn and I exchanged glances. He gave me a nod. So I told Heart about what happened in Afghanistan and about the Mourner ensconced in the safe at my house.

I twisted to face my sister in the backseat. "It's my fault Evie was shot. That bullet was meant for me."

Heart came back at me like the logical older sister I knew. "Don't be ridiculous, Maya. Everything isn't about you. This wacko," she stressed with a glance toward the back of Jorn's head, "is pissed about being left for dead and he wants payback, not to mention the return of his family heirloom."

Jorn remained silent. Heart's no-nonsense view of the world settled my racing mind. My sister was on my side, as always, as much as she might pretend to dislike it. And what few people knew about Heart was: when my sister got mad, she could create hell on earth.

We sprinted through the parking garage, down the underground tunnel leading to the hospital, then up the stairs to the fourth floor, the elevators being too slow. It was eleven o'clock at night, and the corridors were quiet, except for nurses slipping in and out of rooms. The nurse's station on Evie's floor was vacant so we didn't even slow until we skidded to a halt at the door to Evie's room.

Heart and I rushed to Evie's side. We listened to her even breaths, the blessed machine confirming she was alive. I wanted to kiss it. Heart stroked Evie's cheek and whispered over and over, "You're okay. You're okay." She looked at me across our sleeping mother. As our fears slowly faded into relief, I gave her a small reassuring smile.

Larry jumped to his feet. "Girls? What's wrong?"

Jorn stepped forward and placed a hand on Larry's shoulder. "Nothing, Larry."

"Then why are you all here? Maya, you're supposed to be with your grandmother at that religious hootenanny."

I gently released Evie's hand and walked around the bed to Larry. "Gran's with David. And we're here because of this." I showed him the text message and image.

"Who is that?" Larry demanded. "And how did he get in here with Evie?"

"Have you been here all evening?" asked Jorn.

"Of course."

"Didn't take a break for coffee?" Jorn persisted.

Larry started to deny it then stopped to think. I'd noticed that, here in the hospital, amid his worry for Evie, sometimes my quick-witted father had trouble responding to even the simplest questions. "Wait, I went to the cafeteria for a candy bar."

Heart stepped forward. "Candy bar? What's wrong with the food in that cooler over there?" She pointed across the room.

I frowned at her and nodded toward Larry's confused face. In the dark room, he looked tired and fragile. Heart backed off.

"I had the munchies," Larry said, sounding defensive. "I needed chocolate. I was only gone a few minutes."

Jorn turned to me. "He must have been watching, waiting for the room to empty."

"Who?" Larry asked.

"Him." I pointed to the image on the phone. "Did you see this man tonight?"

Larry studied the phone in my hand and shook his head. "No. What does it mean, 'Next time'?"

Heart folded her arms across her chest. "Maya has some crazy idea that the person who shot Evie was aiming for her."

"For Maya?"

"She thinks this is the shooter, this Gasquet guy."

"This man with Evie?" Larry eyes widened, suddenly even more afraid for his wife. He looked around the room, his mind fighting to untangle so many thoughts, to find a handhold of logic in the mist of fear. Suddenly, he stopped and turned to me. "Gasquet? Wait, you had me trace his cell phone. The guy in Afghanistan. He's still sending you messages?"

Jorn filled in Larry on the messages and the fact that we believed Gasquet was here in Minnesota. "We don't know what he wants, but Maya and I are looking for him."

"And now we're looking for him," Heart said with a note of satisfaction, nodding toward Larry, who at last had another mission. Already he was back in his chair, laptop flipped open, and typing like crazy.

Larry mumbled as his fingers danced across the keys. "That bastard. Thinks he can threaten my Evie and my kids? I'll find his sorry ass."

Heart began to pace. "I can't believe just anyone can waltz in here. What kind of hospital is this? Doesn't this place have *any* security?"

I recognized Heart's outraged mother tone, the one she used to annihilate the school administration when it claimed ketchup was a vegetable in the school lunch program. There was a streak of the crusader in my sister, too, and it had come to the party.

She stopped in front of our father. "Larry, we need to contact hospital security. And get this photo to the police investigating the shooting back in Gabriel's Garden."

Larry didn't look up from the keyboard. "I'm on it. I need quiet and chocolate."

"I got the chocolate," Jorn said.

"I got the quiet," I said and tugged my sister toward the door. Heart started to argue, but I simply shook my head. She gave me an annoyed look. I'd had years of handling that expression and just pulled her out of the room.

While Jorn fetched Larry two Snickers bars, Heart and I went to the lounge. Except for a woman knitting in the corner, we were alone. Heart paced. I unrolled Jorn's yoga mat and began to flow through combinations of asanas. I found myself returning to the Warrior poses again and again. I would need the fury of Sati and the single-mindedness of Shiva to protect my family.

"You know he's in there hacking the hospital's security system, right?" Heart stopped in front of my mat for a moment, then began striding up and down the dimly lit room again. Even though my sister had been raised by two people who didn't trust authority and didn't hesitate to twist the law for the common good—the common good being, in this case, our family—she sought to lead the life of an upstanding citizen. She had made peace with Larry's questionable activities, but that didn't mean she had to like them. An upright citizen reported a crazy killer running loose.

I let my sister rant. "This is not fun and games anymore, Maya. You and Jorn playing detective." She stopped in front of me again and pointed to the hall. "Our mother is fighting for her life down there. We need real detectives finding this guy. Now."

I knew she was right. Maybe there was no excuse for not

bringing the police in, since we now had a direct link between Evie and Gasquet.

"You're right," I said.

"You always try to handle things by yourself and—" She stopped in mid-sentence, her mouth snapping shut. She looked at me with suspicion. "You'll send the selfie to the police?"

"It'll lead to questions. Jorn won't like it. All the poking into his life."

"Someone almost killed Evie. That trumps privacy in my book."

When Jorn joined us, I told him that I was giving the selfie to the cops. Slumped in the chair next to the mat where I sat in lotus, he didn't say anything for a while. Finally, he nodded. "Okay, but we'll have to tell them everything. They'll want to question his family, René and Madame Dubois, about their last contact with Gasquet. And we have to be prepared for all of this to drive Gasquet underground again. He's been like smoke."

Gasquet's elusiveness puzzled me. It was difficult to disappear without help; I knew from experience. So who was helping Gasquet?

JORN, HEART, AND I spent the night at the hospital. We took shifts sitting with Evie. Larry was bent over the laptop for most of the night, except when he stretched his long, flannel-clad arms over his head, snapped his spine, and demanded another candy bar.

On one of my shifts sitting in the chair beside Evie's bed,

I pulled from my satchel the bottle Grandmother Sylvia had given me. I poured a drop of the holy oil on the handkerchief and gently placed the handkerchief inside Evie's hospital gown over her heart. After I stoppered the bottle and put it away, I stretched my palm across Evie's chest, on top of the handkerchief, and offered the assistance of reiki, as I had done so many times in the past days. Once again, I felt the warmth growing, seeking. No matter how lifeless Evie appeared, there was life stirring inside her. I knew it; I felt it. This yearning spark kept my hope alive.

As my hand warmed on Evie's chest, I placed my head on her shoulder and whispered, "Mom, come back."

HOURS LATER, I WOKE to bright light streaming into Evie's room and loud tapping at the window. The crow was back, on the ledge as usual. My vigil was its vigil. I rubbed the bracelet on my left arm, the silver cuff Tum the shaman had always worn and I now wore. On it were four symbols: a spiral for man's connection to all things, a turtle to bring good health, a tree of life, and a bird of magic. I got up, stretched my stiff back, and did a few Sun Salutations. As I moved, I thought about the bracelet and the waiting crow and my friend Tum. Tum had believed he was like the crow—that he had transcended his violent Hell's Angels past, lifted himself, and flown into the peaceful life of Whispering Spirit. I had to believe that, like Tum, Evie would rise above her circumstances, this limbo she was caught in. Evie had to survive; I didn't care whether it happened by magic or modern science.

Larry snorted. He was slumped uncomfortably in his

chair. I touched his shoulder, and his eyes immediately snapped open and found Evie. Without a word, I went out to the lounge and woke Heart and Jorn, who were sprawled in strange configurations on the lounge furniture. We all returned to Evie's room.

Larry had his laptop open. "Here's the footage from last night's security tapes. Not much help. He kept his head down. Came in through the garage. Made his way through the hospital easily."

Jorn and I leaned forward, desperate to get a good look at Gasquet.

I asked Jorn, "Is it him? Same walk, same height? If he is so set on taunting us, why is he hiding his face?"

Jorn thought for a moment. "I don't know."

Nothing felt right about this.

"Well, I know one thing," said Heart. "A dead man doesn't walk."

CHAPTER 22

AN UNINVITED PRAYER

O N WEDNESDAY MORNING, PAULETTE and Pavel arrived at the hospital, a thousand miles from their brownstone in Queens. They gathered Larry into their arms—into Paulette's skinny, flabby limbs and Pavel's strong, rib-bending hugs.

"We come. We help," said Pavel with a big smile, pumping Larry's hand then pulling him into another bear hug.

Paulette, who in her penny loafers rose only to the height of one of Pavel's biceps, shouldered the brawny Pavel aside and searched Larry's face. "How ya doin', sugar?"

Larry just shook his head and motioned toward Evie.

Paulette stepped over to Evie's side. She eyed with a frown

the ventilator pushing air into her friend, the tubes snaking into Evie's body, the bars of the hospital bed. We couldn't help but see the bond between the two women, the reverence and pain of a mother for an injured child.

Clearing his throat, eager to lighten the mood of the room, Pavel filled the silence. "Is long way here."

Without taking her eyes off Evie, Paulette agreed, "More than twenty hours. Gawd."

Pavel nodded. "We borrow van from friend. Darling like trip."

"She terrorized every rest stop from home to here," Paulette said softly, absently. Leaning closer to Evie, their cheeks nearly touching, she gently stroked the bandage wrapped around Evie's head. Her voice caught. "Sugar, what did you get yourself into now?"

WHILE JORN DROVE HEART back to Gabriel's Garden to resupply her coolers and catch a nap, I went with Paulette to take Darling the cheetah for a walk. In the dark parking garage, Paulette tugged on the sliding door of a baby blue van. It was an older model, made when happy colors for vehicles were in style. Darling rose at the sound of Paulette's voice.

"Let's take a walk, Darlin'," said Paulette, reaching for a leash. The big cat purred and butted Paulette's arm with her head.

The inside of the van looked and smelled lived in: clothes tossed around, blankets nudged into nests (by Darling probably), maps and packages of cigarettes on the dashboard, and several books (Pavel's presumably) scattered on the floor. I inhaled whiffs of big cat, fried food, and smoke.

Darling elegantly leapt out of the van despite her bum leg. The ridge of the cat's back came up to Paulette's hip. Darling probably outweighed the one-hundred-pound Paulette by a good ten pounds. We walked out of the parking garage and down several blocks to the riverfront. The day was overcast, making the Mississippi below us seem darker and deeper. Paulette lit a cigarette pulled from a fanny pack at her waist.

"She's going to be fine," said Paulette.

I said nothing.

Paulette blew smoke into the air, her bony fingers clutching the cigarette in one hand and Darling's leash in the other. "Your mom's a survivor."

I glanced at her, not sure if she was trying to reassure me or herself.

I told her about our suspicions about Gasquet, but she oddly didn't seem concerned about finding him or bringing him to justice.

"Life is what it is, sugar. And revenge is just plain tiring."

Darling walked between us with a casual wildness. A man sitting on a park bench, his ragtag belongings piled all around him, moved his garbage bags closer and warned, "Keep that big dog away from my stuff."

A runner sprinted around us, giving us a wide berth. Paulette mumbled to Darling, "No." At my puzzled look, Paulette explained, "She loves chasing running things. It's in her blood."

When a police officer stopped us and asked about

Darling, Paulette told him the cheetah was her "emotional-support companion." She tugged a card from the fanny pack and showed it to him.

The officer examined the card closely, looked again at Darling, sitting quietly near Paulette's penny loafers, then handed the card back.

"And it does what for you?"

"Keeps me from going crazy," Paulette said.

He gave her a wary look, issued instructions to keep Darling on a leash and to "clean up after it." Then he continued through the narrow park winding high on a bluff above the Mississippi.

I shook my head at Paulette. "Darling is not an emotional-support animal."

Paulette grinned. "Ordered that little card on the Internet. Only seventy bucks. Legally, it don't mean diddly. But most people don't know that. Gets us into restaurants, ball games, stores."

"But there are people who need real service animal companions. You're abusing the system and ruining it for everyone."

"I know," she said with a grin lacking all remorse. "I'm terrible."

After settling Darling back in her travelling home with a dozen raw hamburgers and filling a large stainless steel bowl with water from one of several gallon jugs stored in the van, we returned to the hospital and found that David had arrived with Grandmother. He also had brought a large vase of cut flowers: lilies, coneflowers, delphiniums. "They're from Evie's garden. I thought she'd like something familiar," he said, giving me a quick smile. David did stuff like this—think of the nonessential things that really were essential. In my sister's precise and orderly world, David infused a tender silliness. He tried so hard to understand the rest of us. Whether we were hunting vortexes or hugging a sick tree to give it healing energy, David tried. And for that, we adored him.

As I walked David to the elevator, he said, "Larry seems a bit edgy."

Larry had grown increasingly grouchy since Gasquet's visit, and being unable to track Gasquet's phone because the GPS was disabled hadn't sweetened his disposition.

I gave David a hug. "He wants to lock up the guy who did this and throw the key in Lake Superior."

"Don't we all?" asked David, returning my hug. Then he left to drive back to Gabriel's Garden. Summer was peak time for the landscaping business in Minnesota.

On my way back to Evie's room, I passed through the lounge, where Pavel and Paulette were camped out, already napping in chairs in the corner. They'd driven through the night to reach their friends. Paulette was curled up, her head on Pavel's lap. I let them sleep and slipped into Evie's room where the scene I found there stopped me in my tracks.

Gran had drawn up a chair close to Larry's. She had her arm around her son—the first time I'd ever seen them touch—and she was whispering to him. Larry's head drooped with exhaustion. I listened.

"I know what it's like to lose someone you love, Lawrence. It's not pretty or easy, but it's—doable."

"She's my heart, Mother."

"I know. I suppose I've always known—from the day she walked through the door."

"But then why—" Larry's head lifted. "You haven't been very nice to her, Mother."

"What did you expect me to do, Lawrence? Give her a prize?"

"I'm tired, Mother. I don't know what I'll do if—" Larry's voice broke. I'd seldom seen Larry cry. Just the sound set off a mantra in my head.

Gran pulled his head closer to her shoulder. "Rest, Lawrence. I'll look after your Evie."

And with that I quietly edged my way back out of the room filled with flowers from Evie's garden, get-well drawings from Evie's granddaughter, and a perhaps a new bond between Evie's mother-in-law and the man Evie loved.

THAT AFTERNOON THE DOCTORS took Evie away for a while for some tests and returned with the news that the swelling around her brain had lessened.

"Will you wake her up?" Larry asked eagerly.

"That's the plan, eventually," said one of the best neurosurgeons in the Midwest, a physician considered to be an inspired healer.

"Then our prayers have been answered," said a voice. We all turned toward the door and found Madame Dubois and René. Although it wasn't Madame Dubois. It was Sister MJ from the looks of her—she wore another silk shirtwaist dress, a different Hermès scarf artfully caressing her neck and shoulders, and the ornate cross that neither Madame Dubois nor Sister MJ were ever without.

"Who's she?" Paulette whispered beside me. From the way Pavel stepped closer to Paulette, I could tell he had heard the same thing I had in Paulette's voice: an immediate dislike of Sister MJ. Larry looked bewildered. Grandmother rose slowly from her chair.

The doctor excused himself as our visitor stepped into the room and introduced herself to Larry. Sandwiching Larry's palm between both of her hands, she said, "Sister MJ."

Larry eased his hand from her grip and stepped back.

"I wanted to come and offer my assistance to your family." She smiled at all of us, lingering for a moment too long on my face. I had noticed that her accent was more pronounced as Madame Dubois. Sister MJ had cultivated an engaging understanding in her syllables. "Perhaps you would allow me to pray with you."

"Who are you?" Larry asked. "Are you the hospital chaplain?"

Grandmother moved beside him, smoothing the front of her Chanel jacket. "No, Lawrence, Sister MJ is ministering at the tent show. Maya and I saw her the other night."

Larry looked shocked as Sister MJ bowed her head and without preamble began. "Lord, we ask You to place Your healing hands on this loving child, Evangeline. She is Your good warrior, struck down, so senselessly."

I glanced at Grandmother. She was studying Sister MJ with calculating eyes.

Sister MJ continued, "I had a vision that something like this would occur."

"What?" Larry was having difficulty taking in Sister MJ.

Sister MJ lifted her head and gave Larry a sad smile. "I didn't know it would be your wife, monsieur. I am so sorry. I surely would have warned you. But sometimes my visions are—not easily interpreted."

Grandmother harrumphed. "Doesn't make them very useful then, does it?"

"I trust in God to provide the key to their meaning." Sister MJ sighed. "Alas, sometimes the key comes too late."

"Or not at all," said Gran.

"I sense your skepticism, madame. I invite you back to the tent revival. Many are spreading the Word there, including myself. I would be pleased to have you join me, to let me show you the path to salvation."

My grandmother straightened her jacket again. "I *know* the path."

"Really?" Sister MJ approached Evie's bed and laid a hand on her arm.

"Hey," Larry objected and would have pulled Sister MJ away if Gran hadn't shaken her head slightly. She had this.

Sister MJ stared at Evie. "We all need the Lord's guidance."

Grandmother wasn't backing down, even though she was throwing down with an internationally renowned warrior of the Lord. "I have the Bible—not some visions—as my guide." That was certainly rich—Grandmother questioning Sister MJ's conduit to the Almighty when Gran admitted to having her own two-way conversations with the Great Spirit.

I couldn't take my eyes off Sister MJ's hand on Evie's arm. It was not a young hand, but it was a well-cared-for one, the skin smooth and the nails polished in a pale pearl pink. It slid down my mother's arm to her hand. And after a few moments, I saw Evie's hand twitch. I couldn't believe it. My eyes flew to Evie's face, which remained as unresponsive as before. I glanced around the room, but the others hadn't noticed the tiny movement. Finally, I looked at Sister MJ and saw a sly smile flit across her face. She *had* noticed.

When Sister MJ stepped back from Evie and turned to Larry, the smile was gone. "I meant no offense," she said. "I just felt that I was needed here today, to give comfort to Maya and her family."

At Sister MJ's familiarity, both Gran and Larry gave me puzzled looks, which I ignored. I kept my attention on Sister MJ.

The whole time, René, who'd been standing in the doorway, had not said a word. Now, he moved to touch Sister MJ's elbow. "We should give them their privacy, *Maman.*"

Sister MJ nodded. She turned to me. "Until next time?"

Her choice of words was like a dunk in an icy river. Stunned, I watched Sister MJ sweep from the room.

In the silence that followed, Larry said, "Who or what was *that*?"

"That," I said, "was Gasquet's mother."

CHAPTER 23

YOGA AND
THE ELEPHANT

JAMES TUMBLETHORNE, THE SHAMAN with a crow tattoo on his shoulder, once told me that not all birds remember their families. Most scatter after leaving the nest without an adieu and wouldn't recognize a mother, father, sister, or brother if they landed on the same tree. But crows are different. They recognize familial ties, the bonds that spin us into happiness and tug us into the abyss, the connections that make us do things we can't explain.

Some of my inexplicable ties were resting in my bedroom. Heart and David were at the hospital with Evie for the night. Paulette and Pavel were bunking at my parents' house and had persuaded Larry to go home with them to, as Paulette put it, "get at least one good night of shut-eye because you look like warmed-over roadkill." Paulette was a small tornado when it came to getting her way, and she had swept Larry up despite his squawks and protests and shuffled him into the back of the van with Darling. That left me with Sadie and Gran, nestled together with Bella in my comfortable bed while I made do on the living room sofa.

It was not easy putting Grandmother down for the night. Halfway up the spiral staircase to my apartment, she offered to buy me an elevator. As I handed out toothbrushes, she complained that old firehouses were drafty, even in August. Testing the bed, she told Sadie she was absolutely not sleeping with a cat.

"Of course, you are," Sadie replied, clutching Bella to her chest. I watched from the doorway as they argued and fought over the blankets and, in the end, as my stubborn grandmother slipped her arm around her equally stubborn great-granddaughter. I quietly closed the bedroom door with a sense of rightness.

Back in the living room, the red sofa did not call me, but the bookshelves did. I crossed the room, tripped the hidden lever, and stood back as the bookshelves swung open. I punched in the code on the keypad and pressed my thumb against the biometric scanner unlocking the door to the safe. I hesitated. Inside, wrapped in Al Jorn's old tartan scarf, was one of the Mourners—Jorn and I were sure of that now. When John the Fearless's tomb was dismantled in 1793 during the French Revolution, some of the Mourner sculptures vanished in the turmoil. And somehow this Mourner had ended up in the coffers of Madame Dubois's family, where it had remained, a family secret, for centuries; never to be reunited with its fellow Mourners in the museum in Dijon. Now we were hiding this artifact of incalculable monetary and historic value. I didn't know why we just didn't return it to Madame Dubois.

Giving in to the pull of the Mourner's energy, I carefully removed the bundled sculpture from the safe and, grabbing the Down Dog Diary from my satchel, went downstairs to the yoga studio. There I lit several candles, the only light in the room, and settled on my yoga mat. My breath caught as I unwrapped the bundle. The smooth white alabaster was exquisite in its detail and begged to be touched. I wanted to trace the folds of the choirboy's robe, the curls of his hair, the creamy contours of his cheek. But I resisted the temptation. I placed Gasquet's Mourner in front of me, always making sure that it was protected from my touch by the scarf. I knew, from countless discussions about art with Evie, that the human finger is full of destructive oils. Our touch can be deadly to such timeless creations.

Then, I opened the diary.

A strong, unpleasant chemical smell drifted from a random page, and I stopped. The entry read: *They say courage is facing one's fear. No, the trick is to simply carry on, let the fear nibble at you and try to eat you alive. Carry on and courage will fill you where fear has hollowed you out.*

I closed my eyes and deepened my breathing. The nothingness of meditation had always been my friend, my guide to answers. In stress, my mantras kicked in, but they could only take me so far. The real work was always done here on the mat—the business of balance, the job of letting stillness and insight come. Here in the nothingness is where I carried on and waited, waited to be filled with courage. My mind turned over Sister MJ's last words, "Until next time?" Was it coincidence—Sister MJ speaking nearly the same words as were on Gasquet's selfie—or was she in contact with Gasquet? And if she was, then why ask us to find him? What game was she playing? Was she protecting a son who had come back from that last assignment a changed man, no longer the loving son and trusted friend?

Jorn and I had wondered how Gasquet knew we would be at the art museum on that Sunday in July. Maybe we were not the main attraction. What if Gasquet had really come to see the Mourners, to be close to the brothers of the family heirloom he had lost by a technicality? Maybe, Gasquet truly had been unable to communicate with his lawyers as scheduled and they had made a mistake, accidentally activating his post-mortem instructions when he wasn't dead yet. If only I had been able to see the face under the hoodie—was Gasquet more interested in Jorn or the Mourners, in revenge or family duty?

On the other hand, it made sense that, in case of his demise, Gasquet would trust the sculpture to Jorn and no one else. The man in Jorn's stories, the artist, would have felt compelled to return this historic relic to its rightful place and knew Jorn, a seeker of truth, would see that it was done. So why was Jorn holding on to lost treasure?

I don't know how long I sat there. No answers surfaced from the nothingness, forcing their way to the top like a glistening gift. Sometimes this inner work was stubborn. It would have its way when it was ready. I knew better than to push, but nothing had seemed clear or right since I first saw Evie in that hospital bed. I opened my eyes and found another pair of eyes staring at me out of the dark.

It was Sadie. Sitting in lotus, opposite of me, patient and silent. I smiled into her sober face, but there was no answering grin. She remained unmoving, a statue here on business. "Have you given Granny Evie reiki?" she asked. I'd used this Japanese healing technique on a tree in Sadie's yard when it was dying, and somehow it had survived.

I nodded. "Yes."

"Then why isn't she getting better?" my niece demanded.

"We don't know she isn't. Only the Universe knows."

"I want her to come home. Now."

"Me too."

She reached for the sculpture standing between us. I stopped her with a shake of my head. She sat back, tilted her head in question: "Isn't this like the happy Buddha?" She glanced at the table behind us to the Buddha, whose big belly invited the touch of those seeking good fortune. He was a jolly fellow, a man of little means meant to remind us of how contentment is not found in the outer world of things but inside of us, in our nothingness.

"No," I said. "It's not meant to be touched. It's precious and old. One of the Mourners from the Court of Burgundy."

"Where is that?"

"France."

Sadie's eyes brightened with interest. If it was from France, it was worthy of her attention.

"Long ago, a prince in France hired artists to build a grand tomb for him," I said. "He ordered them to create forty sculptures like this one. It took the artists years. The sculptures represented the eternal grief of the people for the loss of their prince. It showed he was a man of importance."

"It sounds like he had a big head."

"That too."

"And it isn't very nice, is it? To *want* people to be sad."

Sadie and I considered the beautiful Mourner for a long time. The melting candles cast shadows over Sadie's face, which was as smooth as the alabaster choirboy's. By now it was early morning, a time for whispering fears, and Sadie moved over beside me on my mat.

In a halting voice, she ambushed me. "Is Granny Evie going to die?" There it was, the thought we had all been shoving back into the closet and running from. The elephant had tiptoed into the room.

"I don't know," I whispered.

In a soft voice, Sadie said, "Mama says I should pray to Spirit. But I don't think Spirit listens all the time."

I wasn't going to lie; I never lied to Sadie. "Yes, sometimes it seems our prayers are just going into the air. That is how faith works. We send something out into the Universe, believing it will help but not really knowing for sure."

Sadie frowned. "I don't like it."

Of course, she didn't. Response was an absolute in Sadie's life. The members of her family had never been too busy not to address her needs. Maybe that was the privilege of being an only child and only grandchild—a mother and father always willing to set things right, a grandfather who would stop everything to answer a question, an aunt who couldn't say no. Only Evie demanded loving independence from her granddaughter—and patience. She kept our dear Sadie from being utterly spoiled.

I told her, "A friend of mine used to say that Spirit talks to us when we're willing to listen."

Sadie's brow wrinkled. "I don't get it."

"Sometimes I don't either," I admitted.

Leaning against me, Sadie announced with a tired sigh, "For smart people, we can be pretty dumb."

Despite the hour and knowing my sister would not approve if she knew her daughter was practicing yoga in the middle of the night, I said, "Go get a mat."

Then, mats spread side by side, we flowed from one pose to another, together. Although Heart refused to come to yoga classes, Larry and Evie had been bringing Sadie to yoga since she was a baby. As we moved with the breath, my mind filled with a memory of Evie in Warrior Pose, one arm stretched behind her and the other clasped around six-month-old Baby Sadie, who was balanced on Evie's bent front leg. I could almost hear Evie laughing and Sadie gurgling.

I told Sadie how she and Evie used to practice Warrior. The memory lit her. And, suddenly, there it was—that Baby Sadie grin, coming out of the darkness, filling my heart with contentment. Whatever happened, we had that moment and this one.

Finally, we folded into Child's Pose, curled, relaxed, and breathed. Our foreheads on the mat, we reached our arms out before us. Sadie turned her head and our eyes met. "Will the person who hurt Granny Evie try again?"

Before I could answer, an imperious voice from the doorway said, "Of course not."

It was Grandmother wrapped in my robe, the one with penguins frolicking all over it. Underneath, I knew, she wore nothing but her old-fashioned slip. We'd all been too tired to stop for pajamas.

Sadie leaned back and sat up on her knees. "Are you sure?" she asked, her tone as haughty as her great-grandmother's.

"I am sure of many things. One is that young girls should be in bed at this time of night."

Sadie stood, rolled up her mat, and went back to bed. Head cocked, Gran listened to Sadie's footsteps on the spiral stairs, then turned to me. "Older ones, too."

THE NEXT MORNING, THURSDAY, Jorn was knocking on my door with coffee for him, tea for me, and a bag of chocolate-chip muffins from Northern Lights. Hallie, the owner of the only coffee shop in Gabriel's Garden, baked a mouth-watering muffin made purely of Fair Trade and organic ingredients. She was a woman with a Whispering Spirit heart and the skill of a gourmet chef.

Sadie and Gran heard us and wandered out from the bedroom, both with bed head. Sadie yawned, spotted the Northern Lights bag, and pounced on it. "Muffins!"

"Coffee," Grandmother sighed, lifting Jorn's cup out of his hand as she passed him and settling into a kitchen chair with a groan. Sadie had already spread two paper napkins on the table as plates, one for her and one for Gran. She placed a large muffin in the center of each.

Jorn looked from my roommates to me.

"Sleepover," I explained.

His eyes followed his coffee, the one Gran was sipping with pleasure.

Her mouth full, Sadie said, "Great-Gran snores."

"A lady never snores," Gran told Sadie, brushing a muffin crumb from her Chanel skirt. "She dreams with vigor. And you kick."

"I sleep with vigor," Sadie retorted.

I handed my tea to Jorn, since Gran had absconded with his morning wake-up. He frowned at it with disgust and slid it onto the counter when he thought I wasn't looking. I pretended I didn't see.

None of us appeared to be at our best, not even the weather. Outside, the sky was dreary, and raindrops slid down the windowpane. Days like this were unpredictable. They could spoil your plans and an hour later lift them with a shot of surprising sunshine. As Larry always said, "If you don't like Minnesota weather, just wait a minute."

Sadie requested hot chocolate so I put on the tea kettle. Jorn sidled next to me at the stove. "Can we talk?" he asked in a low voice. I glanced over my shoulder at Sadie and Gran who were arguing about the ingredients of a proper breakfast.

"Lawrence ate oatmeal every day of his childhood, and it didn't hurt him," Gran said.

"Oatmeal is old," Sadie said. "We have modern food now. Pop-Tarts and pizza." I grinned to myself, as if Heart would ever let Sadie eat a Pop-Tart or pizza for breakfast.

I told Gran and Sadie we would be right back and asked them to watch the kettle. Jorn snatched my laptop from the sofa and followed me downstairs to the studio. He placed the computer on the table next to Buddha, tapped the laptop into life, and began Googling. In moments, he had found what he was looking for: a report on a correspondent who had been beheaded by terrorists somewhere in the Middle East. The still photo, taken from a gruesome video, showed a man dressed in orange, kneeling in the desert, and the masked executioner, all in black, waving a rather ordinary-looking knife, not much longer than a butcher's blade.

This had become a far too regular occurrence—men and women of the press being used as pawns in propaganda. But Jorn knew from personal experience that being a journalist in areas of conflict was an iffy proposition. How was this case different?

When I saw the expression on Jorn's face, I realized, "You knew him, didn't you?"

Jorn nodded. "He was freelance like me. Like Gasquet." Jorn paused, caught in memories of days living abroad on assignment and the camaraderie of men and women far from home all doing the same thing: searching for the truth. "Sometimes we'd meet up in a café, share a drink. He was one of those guys who always found something to laugh about, no matter how shitty the circumstances. Liked to show us pictures of his kid back in the States." Jorn rubbed his face. He looked tired. "I liked him."

A sound from the door had us turning. It was Gran with two steaming cups of hot chocolate. She handed a cup to each of us and studied the scene on the computer screen.

"In my day," she said, "journalists were like Switzerland. Neutral. People respected that. Can't imagine Edward R.

Murrow without his head." She tapped Jorn on the arm. "You going back there?"

Jorn shrugged. "I don't know."

"Well, if you do, hang on to your head." And with that, Gran left us.

The ghost of a smile flit across Jorn's face as he watched my grandmother slowly make her way across the studio floor. After sniffing his cup, he took a sip. "Gasquet never took that decapitation shit seriously. He thought he was an artist and that artists had some hall pass when it came to the real world."

"And you?"

"There are no rules in war. I never expected there to be any."

"But Gasquet was different."

"I was after story; he was after art. He'd do nearly anything for the perfect shot."

"A daredevil?"

"Yeah, sometimes he took risks, got too close to the action. But he never risked my life or the lives of others."

Obviously, the Gasquet of then did not mesh with the Gasquet of now. Surely, Jorn had to see that. Something had changed; his friend had changed. Jorn touched the happy Buddha's belly. "We have to find Gasquet. Talk to him. He needs our help."

Help? I wanted to say, he shot my mother; I'll give him help all right. But I didn't. Instead, I sipped my hot chocolate and glanced out at the rainy day.

"Why didn't you go back to look for Gasquet after you got out of the hospital?"

Jorn didn't answer. I turned and found him staring at the floor, a look of uncertainty on his face. His hand was rubbing his injured hip.

I said carefully, "Are you afraid to go back?"

He didn't look up at me, just kept rubbing that hip. After a while, he whispered, "I'm sorry I left him."

"Anyone would be afraid," I told him.

"But how could I . . . I thought he was dead."

The rain and the video of Jorn's friend sealed the room in gloom. I lowered the laptop lid, sending the computer back into hibernation, and set my cup beside it. I stepped toward Jorn, reached up, and touched his cheek. It was bristly. He hadn't shaved or, from the look of the shadows under his eyes, slept much either. After a pause, he leaned into my hand and closed his eyes. I shoved the images from the laptop from my mind and focused on sending loving energy to Jorn. We stayed that way, listening to the rain.

Finally, I cleared my throat and steered us away from pain and memory to the safer ground of investigation. "Madame Dubois paid a visit to Evie yesterday," I said.

Jorn leaned back, frowned. "What did she want?"

"She came as Sister MJ to pray for Evie's recovery."

"Weird."

"She said something—"

"What?"

I repeated Sister MJ's parting words. Jorn immediately recognized them and tensed.

His eyes searched mine. "She knows where he is. She's talked to him," he said, disbelief in his voice.

"It's beginning to look that way."

This news set Jorn pacing. "All this time—" His footsteps rang in the empty room. "Return my son to me. Have Gasquet send me a postcard."

"What should we do?"

"Have a little chat with Madame Dubois."

"Do you really think she'll tell us anything?"

"I've cracked nuts tougher than she is."

I picked up my cup, sipped hot chocolate that had grown cold, and smiled to myself. This was the old Jorn; the truth seeker had come out to face the storm. A Jorn on the scent was better than one cowering in a cave of guilt.

"I've been wondering," I said, "why don't we just give the sculpture back to Gasquet's family?"

Jorn stopped pacing. "The Mourner?"

I watched him over the rim of my cup. "We have no business keeping it. It's a national treasure. So what the hell are we doing with it?"

"Madame Dubois and René are certainly eager to have it back." His eyes avoided mine.

"Either you don't trust them—"

"Turns out I was right."

"Or," I said, "you're using the Mourner as bait to draw Gasquet to you."

A sheepish grin slipped across Jorn's face, followed by a shrug. "Uncle Al always said I was a lousy fisherman."

CHAPTER 24

DENIAL IS NOT A RIVER; IT'S A DEEP SEA WITH MONSTERS

THE STORM HAD MOVED on, leaving behind overcast skies and air heavy with moisture. The Strawberry B&B's baskets of petunias and verbenas glistened with raindrops. As Jorn and I climbed the porch steps, Helen the proprietor was wiping down the rockers on the front porch. We asked for Madame Dubois. She pointed inside and said, "Salon. That's a favorite on rainy mornings."

We entered the Strawberry's shadowy foyer, where a large crystal vase of yellow roses sat on an antique side table. The flowers' perfume mixed with the delicious smells of that morning's breakfast, and I realized I hadn't eaten. The muffins had been gone by the time we got back upstairs.

We found Madame Dubois and René seated on a floral sofa in the inn's comfy salon. René was reading something on his tablet, and Madame Dubois was studying a well-used Bible. They stood as we approached.

"Peter. Maya." Madame Dubois held out her hands. As we neared, she pulled each of us toward her in turn and kissed both cheeks. René also gave us the customary greeting then lightly held his mother's elbow, helping her back into her seat. She waved us toward the chairs opposite the sofa. "You have news. I can tell. Sit, sit."

"Yes," René said. "What news?"

I leaned back in the chair and studied Madame Dubois. Was she conspiring with her son Gasquet? What did a collaborator look like? Her dress was simple and chic, her smile was inviting not nervous, and her eyes met ours with interest and openness. René was relaxed as well, his legs crossed at the knee, his smile friendly.

Jorn leaned forward, his eyes intent. "Madame Dubois, we have some questions."

"Questions? But, of course, Peter, we will help in any way we can."

"You said that you haven't seen Gasquet for nearly a year."

"That is correct."

"And yet you said something yesterday to Maya at the hospital that was almost the exact words recently used by Gasquet."

"I don't understand."

Jorn pulled his smartphone from his jacket, scrolled to

a message, and showed the phone to Madame Dubois. It was the selfie of Gasquet. She gasped, snatched the phone from his hand, and stared at it. "Gasquet," she whispered. She leaned closer to René and showed him the image. He unfolded his legs and together they huddled over the phone. Madame Dubois's face shone with new hope. She clutched the phone to her chest for a moment before giving it back to Jorn.

Even though we had sent a copy of the text and image to the police yesterday, this appeared to be the first time the Duboises had seen it. What would Madame Dubois say when the police finally did get around to questioning her and she learned that Gasquet was a person of interest in the shooting of my mother?

Jorn pointed to the phone. "Madame, see the text under the image? They are almost the exact same words that you said to Maya in the hospital."

Madame Dubois ignored Jorn and turned to her son. "René, your brother is here. He was in that very room where we were."

"*Oui, Maman.*"

Madame Dubois's fingers touched her lips. "He's here," she said in a voice filled with disbelief and anticipation.

Jorn cleared his throat. "The text, madame, what about the text?"

"What?" The woman turned to us, confused, her eyes unfocused.

"The words, 'Next time.'"

René dismissed the point with a chuckle. "It is coincidence, Peter. Merely a phrase."

Like my mentor Tum, I did not believe in coincidence.

"So neither of you has spoken to Gasquet recently?" I asked.

"Spoken to Gasquet?" Madame Dubois looked even more puzzled, her hands began to fidget with the pearl and gold cross at her neck. "I do not understand." Her accent thickened, and René moved closer to her.

"I think you're not telling us everything, madame," Jorn said.

René tensed, slowly rising to his feet. "How dare you—"

Jorn persisted. "Do you know where Gasquet is now, at this very moment, madame?"

Madame Dubois was shaking her head. "*Non, non.*"

"Leave her alone," growled René.

She plucked at René's sleeve, trying to get him to sit back down. "*S'il te plaît*, René, *calme-toi.*"

"*Maman*, he is calling us liars," René ground out.

"I am sure that is not what Peter meant." Her eyes searched Jorn's then mine. "I have not seen my son."

"Madame," said Jorn, "I need to talk to Gasquet. If you have any way to contact him—"

Madame Dubois lifted an elegant shoulder. "But we are as much in the dark as you are, Peter."

"You've had no communication from him or his lawyers then?" Jorn continued.

"Lawyers?" Still standing, a baffled René ran his hand through his close-cropped and carefully styled hair then suddenly stopped. "Wait. Have you heard from Gasquet's lawyers?"

Jorn neither confirmed nor denied.

Madame Dubois touched Jorn's hand, the one still holding the smartphone with the photo of Gasquet in Evie's hospital room. Her gaze was direct. "I have not seen my son for nearly a year, Peter. Why is he in the room with Maya's mother? Why is he playing these games with photographs?" She opened the Bible and pulled out a postcard tucked between the pages. The last postcard sent by Gasquet, I bet. The corners were bent from being handled, read again and again. I couldn't see the writing of the message, but I could make out the date—October, the month Jorn and Gasquet were ambushed. Madame Dubois pressed the card close to her chest, trapping it against the cross dangling from her neck.

"I have not seen my son," she repeated.

And I found myself believing her.

CHAPTER 25

SHE'S ALIVE,
NO WAIT

HEART AND DAVID SENT word that Evie had been taken off the ventilator. That created an exodus to the Cities, a caravan of concern: In Paulette and Pavel's van, I could just imagine Larry, foot jiggling, demanding that Pavel drive faster and Paulette talking calmly to Darling. In my car, Gran prayed in the front seat and Sadie chattered in the back, "This is good news, right?"

When we entered the hospital room, all eyes immediately searched Evie's face. The tubes were gone from her mouth, but otherwise Evie was just the same—still expressionless, still unconscious. You could almost touch the disappointment in the room.

Larry took a jolting step forward and grasped Evie's hand. Sadie skirted around the bed to the other side, leaned close to Evie's ear, and whispered loudly, "Granny Evie, you can wake up now."

There was no response. The room seemed too quiet; I never thought I'd miss that noisy, pumping ventilator, a reassuring sign of life.

Evie's doctor nudged his way through the crowd. He patted Larry on the shoulder. "She's breathing on her own. That's good."

"Then why isn't she waking up?" demanded Sadie, stepping back from the bed, hands on her hips, one eyebrow cocked at the best neurosurgeon in the Midwest.

"We have to wait and let her come out of the coma when she's ready," the doctor told Sadie.

That response did not sit well with my niece. "Great-Gran, do something," she said, turning to Grandmother.

Grandmother just shook her head.

Sadie eyed Heart then me. "Mama. Maya."

Heart, leaning on David, said in a tired voice, "Sadie baby."

"Well, *somebody* has to do something," Sadie cried.

Larry walked around the bed and lifted Sadie into his arms. Wrapping her colt legs around his hips, she buried her face in his shoulder and sobbed. And then I heard softly, lifting from Larry's lips, a familiar lullaby that he'd modified for Sadie and had been singing to her since she first opened her eyes: "St. Judy's Comet."

"O, little sleepy girl . . . "

I glanced at Evie and saw a twitch of the eye. I stepped

closer, tapped the doctor's arm, and nodded toward Evie. "I saw something," I whispered.

He leaned over Evie, listened to her heart, took her vital signs. As he was doing so, he muttered in a low voice, "Involuntary movements." His eye caught mine, and I understood. Obviously, he didn't want to get everyone's hopes up. He was cautious by nature and profession, but I was a creature of hope. I believed in magic, and I would hold that tiny magical movement in my heart for as long as necessary.

FOR THE NEXT TWENTY-FOUR hours, there were no more twitches. I watched for any sign: the fluttering of eyelashes, the lifting of a single finger, the curl of a toe under the blanket. Evie breathed, but she did not wake. She did not squeeze my hand when I squeezed hers. And outside the rain stopped and started just as my heart did every time I imagined I felt some new awareness in my mother. The crow outside the window ruffled its wet feathers, and raindrops cascaded like diamonds. The window ledge offered little protection from the showers that had returned.

"You don't have to stay," I told the crow.

It cocked its head, pecked at the window once, and shook out its feathers again.

It was Friday afternoon, and everyone else was sacked out in the lounge or at home in Gabriel's Garden. I wiggled in the uncomfortable chair beside Evie's bed, searching for a position I hadn't tried in the last hours. Finally, I got up, unrolled Jorn's yoga mat, and began to move on the hard tile floor. As I flowed through Sun Salutation on this sunless day, the crow outside the window bobbed its head. Salutation followed salutation eventually flowing into Warriors; practice evolved into meditation. Soon my mind was nowhere and my breathing was everywhere. The room filled like a balloon with peaceful energy, squeezing out the worry and sadness.

"Oh!" said a voice. "I didn't mean to interrupt . . ."

I stopped and turned toward the red-haired nurse who stood in the doorway with flowers in her hand and an expression of chagrin.

"No problem," I said.

"Oh, well then, here are more flowers for Mrs. Skye." With a smile, she placed the large arrangement of crimson roses near the window. "My husband gives me these every Valentine's Day. They mean true love."

I was not a fan of "days," which, to me, were decorated with gimmicks and smelled entirely too much of commercialism. I avoided them at all costs. But Evie always said "days" were important because they reminded people to be aware, to think of someone besides themselves, to remember and honor. As a child in Whispering Spirit, we honored everything: I Don't Have a Hole in My Sock Day, Bless the Wind Day, Rabbits Left Us One Head of Lettuce Day. Evie had found a way to be grateful for every day. The memories made me smile.

The nurse continued, "These must be from Mr. Skye. He clearly is devoted to her."

Her expression was sympathetic. She had been on duty many days this past week and seen the suffering of my family. I thanked her.

After she was gone, I stepped closer and studied the roses, such a velvety red they seemed unreal. As it often was with flowers, they could symbolize different things in different cultures. The crimson rose was the gift of lovers, but it also represented grief.

The rose, such a formal flower, such an ordinary choice, really wasn't Larry's style at all. I took a step back. In one of the fake diaries, Evie had drawn a daffodil clutched in a set of false teeth. A single daffodil telling me to beware; fake teeth warning of a liar in our midst. It was one of those strange connections Evie often made in her art that no one could explain, not even Evie.

With trepidation, I plucked the card from the arrangement and slid it from the envelope. It said simply: *Gasquet.*

CHAPTER 26

FOLLOW THE SUN

SADIE CAME BOUNCING INTO the room, a ball of energy on a dull day, and I quickly hid Gasquet's card in my pocket. She zeroed in on the roses, stuck her nose into the middle of the bouquet, and inhaled deeply. "Pretty," she said.

Following her daughter, Heart opened the cooler in the corner and transferred ice packs, sandwiches, and bags of healthy munchies from an insulated tote to the cooler. Nodding toward the flowers, she said, "Don't eat those. They're probably poisonous. You don't know what they spray on things these days."

"I wouldn't eat roses." Sadie made a face of exasperation, and we grinned at each other.

Still rummaging in her tote, Heart said in that motherly know-it-all voice, "Once you ate a cricket."

"I was two."

Ignoring that riposte, Heart turned to me, "Any change?"
I shook my head.

She walked to the bed, looked down at Evie, and quietly issued one of her rare curses. "Dammit, Evie, come on." I watched as Sadie stepped beside Heart and reached for her mother's hand. I remembered the cricket incident, how worried Heart the young mother had been and how the unflappable Evie had reassured her that all things that go in eventually come out. And it did, considerably the worse for wear.

I rolled up the yoga mat, and with a kiss to Evie's forehead and hugs for Sadie and Heart, I handed the watch over to my sister.

Sitting in my car in the dim parking garage, I phoned Jorn. He picked up on the first ring.

"Evie got some flowers today," I paused, "from Gasquet."

"You're kidding." From the thoughtful tone of his voice, I could imagine Jorn running through the possible reasons for this new contact. "Do you have the florist name?"

"Yeah, a Saint Paul shop. I'm heading there now."

"Show them Gasquet's picture. Probably paid cash. But maybe he said something that they'll remember, some remark about his hotel or something he saw on the street while driving around."

I knew what he was thinking. We needed any information that would help us pinpoint where Gasquet was hiding out.

I hung up and found the florist shop on Snelling Avenue. Marsala's. A tinkling bell over the door announced my entrance. I stepped into a cloud of earthy smells, a moist jungle of plants trying their hardest to take over the tiny space. As

I made my way to the back of the shop, I glanced from the large refrigerator and the buckets of bursting blooms to the fairy lights dripping from the ceiling and framing the windows. From a back room stepped an elaborately tattooed, caramel-skinned, young woman wearing a huge grin and a batik orange and blue scarf wrapped around her head. Her top edged up above her frayed jeans showing a belly button ring similar to the one I wore.

"Welcome," she said, and happiness rose in me. I couldn't help but return her smile. The woman had the ability to infuse a lightness in others, an Evie quality.

"Are you Marsala?" I asked, pointing to the shop name above the counter.

"Sure am," she said.

I ordered a bouquet of sunflowers for Evie. As Marsala tied the long, thick stems together with a satiny orange bow, she said, "You can't go wrong with something that follows the sun, can you?"

"No," I said, pulling Gasquet's card from my pocket. "I was also wondering if you could tell me anything about this order."

Marsala took the envelope, pulled out the card, flipped it over and back again. Without a decrease in the voltage of her glow, she said, "The envelope is one of mine, but the card is not."

I glanced at the rack of cards on the counter. All were printed with some kind of theme decoration: flowers, baby rattles, crosses, wedding bells. Gasquet's card was on plain but expensive ivory stock, no ornamentation. He had not gotten it here.

Marsala asked, "Was there a problem with the order?"

"No, no. I was just wondering about the man who sent them."

"I don't talk about my customers." Grinning, Marsala leaned closer across the counter. "One never knows if the person asking is the wife or someone not the wife. Get me?"

I smiled in understanding. "That's not the situation here."

Marsala's face took on a serious expression. The room seemed to grow dimmer, as if modulated by Marsala's mood. I glanced at the fairy lights. She lowered her voice, "Is he bothering you?"

"Not like you think." That seemed to relieve Marsala; she had not sold roses to a stalker. Still she hesitated. She was not a natural gossip, and a smart businesswoman kept her business private. "Please," I said, "whatever you can tell me will help. It's a friend, and he's . . . rather lost right now."

After several moments of thought, Marsala gave a nod and tugged off the scarf that was wrapped around her head. Dreadlocks fell in streams down her slender back. "He had hair like mine."

She handed the card back to me. I paid for the sunflowers.

I showed her the photo of Jorn and Gasquet. She nodded and the dreadlocks danced. "That's him, but that's all I can tell you."

I persisted. "Did he say where he was staying? Or talk about any local landmarks?"

But Marsala had decided she'd said enough. She gave me that sweet smile and nothing else.

I made one last try. "Did he pay for the order with a credit card?" I asked.

Marsala tapped a sign on the counter: *No plastic. Checks or cash only, baby.*

Jorn had been right; Gasquet paid for the flowers with cash. There was no trail for Larry to track.

Marsala did tell me one more thing, though, before I left: It wasn't a delivery; Gasquet had picked up the flowers that morning. That meant he had dropped them off at the hospital himself. While I had been practicing yoga at Evie's bedside, he had been steps away.

CHAPTER 27

A FIRE STARTING
IN MY SOUL

FORGIVENESS IS EASIER SAID than done. It is like looking at the mountain ahead, which seems so small and easy—until you get to it. Then there are boulders the size of elephants and bushes with thorns like sabers. And all you can think about is the moment that brought you to this mountain, the event that drove reason from your head and healing from your heart. This fire consumes you, and soon you aren't "you" anymore.

I had been fighting to keep control of this burning inside me ever since that bullet came streaking through the air and slammed into our lives. But when it comes to the harm of a loved one, the human heart can fill with hatred in a flash, and the blaze in mine had been rising for a week. I wanted to find the person who hurt Evie, and I wanted to hurt him. I wanted to reach Gasquet before Jorn. I wanted retribution.

I had been taught better, and I had been taught smarter. In the privacy of the woods far from the rest of the peace-loving Whispering Spirit family, Tum had trained me: how to punch, kick, evade. He'd tutored me on when to fight and when to not. "Self-defense, kid, always," Tum had told me. "You don't have the heart of a hunter."

But I was growing such a heart. Revenge smothered inner peace, and I was mad at Gasquet for his games, at Evie for not waking up, at the Universe for not getting off its ass and fixing this. I wanted to reverse time, to undo these feelings, to return to a life that was even and smooth and to a time when I was fearless. Because now I lived in dread of two things: that no matter what I did to Gasquet it would not quench this burning anger and that Jorn would never forgive me for hurting his friend.

Saturday dawned overcast and heavy again, but dry. I had intended to do something normal, like clean the apartment, before my afternoon shift at the hospital, but I never got farther than the sofa and a pile of mail. I sat in the middle of all the sofa's red energy, drained, legs in lotus, listlessly stroking Bella who was curled in the bowl of my lap. I sorted mail into piles on the low table in front of me: junk, bills, and condolences. Words of kindness and encouragement from students, neighbors, and friends fell into the last pile. As I slit open the envelopes, I remembered the day I'd read Evie her get-well notes at the hospital. Suddenly, the pile of correspondence slipped from my fingers and tumbled onto the rug.

I fumbled in my jeans pocket for the card from Gasquet's flowers, uprooting Bella from her comfortable spot. I stared at the wrinkled card and tapped it against my fingers. The paper was ivory, expensive; the handwriting, florid, beautiful. Something nibbled at my subconscious. I'd seen that handwriting before. Was it in Gasquet's apartment? No. Then where?

It came to me, a bolt of recognition. I jumped up from the sofa, grabbed my tennis shoes, pulled them on as I hopped around the apartment. Snatching my keys and satchel from the counter, I scrambled down the stairs. I started the car with one hand, while rummaging in my satchel for my cell phone with the other. I had to get a hold of Jorn. No phone. I must have left it upstairs. Forget about it. I'll drive over to Jorn's and bang on his door.

We had to move now.

CHAPTER 28

THE WRITING IN THE WOODS

THE HANDWRITING ON MADAME Dubois's card and the card accompanying Gasquet's roses was the same.

We had to find Madame Dubois.

As I drove, Jorn muttered, "She's known where he was all along. She's been lying to us." His disheveled hair looked even crazier than usual. I'd dragged him out of bed and had refused to let him stop for coffee. He was in a charming mood.

He keyed in the number for the Strawberry B&B, had a brief conversation with Ellen, hung up, and tossed his phone on the dash in frustration. "Not at the Strawberry."

"Then she's at the chapel."

"How do you know?"

I shrugged.

"Your blasted intuition again." Jorn slouched in the passenger seat like a sulking teenager. I was regretting not letting him stop at Northern Lights. "I wish just once we had some facts to follow. Is it too much to ask for? Just once, for A to lead to B and B to C?"

"Sounds extremely orderly," I teased.

He gave me a sour look. "You know nothing of good reporting."

I pushed the Subaru to eat up the highway to the Chapel of the Forgiving Heart while Jorn continued to grouse.

"I'd rather face hungry headhunters or corrupt politicians than your intuition. Nothing ever makes sense. What the hell do daffodils, false teeth, and crows have to do with each other? I defy you to draw a straight line."

"I'm more of a scribbler."

"A daffodil is a flower. That's it."

I said, "The false teeth indicate someone's lying. Obviously, it's been Madame Dubois."

"And what about the crows? You know I'm no fan of birds. We see a flock of crows and I'm grabbing you and getting out of Dodge."

"It's murder. Murder of crows."

"We better not see any murders today, either."

We turned onto the gravel road to the chapel just as the sun struggled out of the clouds. I ignored the "No Parking" sign and parked right in front of the church. We surged out of the car, but Jorn paused, peering out at the tents, campers, and RVs in the field beside the church. "He could be hiding in any one of those. Or he could be camping in the woods. He likes roughing it."

I slapped my hand on the top of the car roof to get Jorn's attention and nodded toward the chapel. We climbed the steps together. As I reached for the handle of the door, Jorn stopped me. "Why do I get the feeling we've been led here?"

"Your blasted intuition?" I grinned at him and tugged on the handle of the heavy red door of the Chapel of the Forgiving Heart.

The interior was cool and dim, the only light coming from the candles on the altar and the sun beginning to streak through the eastern windowpanes.

She sat in the middle of the front pew. Alone. The golden light surrounding her like a halo. She looked small in all the emptiness. Without exchanging a word, Jorn and I automatically split. I took the center aisle, and Jorn approached from the side.

As I reached the front of the church, I saw by the clothes that it was Madame Dubois and not Sister MJ we were confronting. No flowing shirtwaister, expensive scarf, and stylish heels. Madame Dubois wore a short, collarless jacket and flowing pants, the first pantsuit I'd ever seen her wear. On her feet were black ankle boots of soft leather, and around her neck was the jeweled cross. I stood for a moment, studying Gasquet's mother. With face lifted to the altar, her eyes on the simple crucifix nailed to the wall, she ignored us.

"Madame," I said quietly. "We've come for the truth."

She did not turn toward me, just kept staring at the cross. I raised my voice. "Madame, where is Gasquet?"

Jorn stepped out of the shadows and drew near, his

footsteps echoing on the plank floor of the chapel. Finally, she broke her focus on the cross. She glanced first at Jorn and then at me. Her hand lifted to the gold necklace. "He is my son," she whispered.

We waited.

Her eyes pleaded with mine. I saw sadness, determination, a sudden resolve. It was time to end this.

"Take us to him, madame," I said, my voice filled with understanding. The devotion to family was stamped into my DNA, too.

She hesitated, then with a nod, rose.

"Follow me."

Together we walked down the center aisle, Jorn bringing up the rear. We passed through strips of light, and I felt as if we were in a tunnel and finally reaching the end. Gasquet.

I pushed open the chapel door and let Madame Dubois proceed first into the clear light of day. She took the lead, out of the church, down the steps, around the side of the building, toward the woods. She nodded at the few who greeted her. It was Saturday morning, and the grounds around the big red tent were curiously quiet. Most people were either sleeping in or running errands before the tent meeting that night. The scene had the feel of lost magic: the sun too bright, the fairy lights gone. It was as if a hole had opened up and drained the energy from the air.

Madame Dubois paused at the entrance to the woods, then without a glance back at us, stretched out her arm, parted the foliage, and stepped through. I entered the woods after her, immediately sensing a new, uneasy stillness. None of us spoke. Her ankle boots, a style I'd never seen on her or Sister MJ before, knew the way, crunching a pine cone here, kicking a stone there. Without pause, she stepped with sureness.

She took us deeper and deeper. I had no idea if we were still on the Reverend Miley's land. At one point, Jorn touched my waist. When I turned to him, he nodded to the right and faded quietly into the undergrowth. He was as nervous as I was. Where was René? And where was Gasquet? Where was Madame Dubois taking us? Better to approach from two fronts than in a vulnerable single file.

The crows were disturbed, setting up a racket at our intrusion, their caws reaching new levels, their wings sweeping through the trees all around us. Madame Dubois stepped easily over a fallen log in the path and broke into an open area, a circle padded with soft pine needles, petite wildflowers, and short grass surrounded by tall, mysterious pine trees and savage oaks. In the middle of the circle, she stopped and turned. In her hand was a gun.

CHAPTER 29

STEPPING INTO THE DARK

AND RIGHT THEN, I knew.

There was no Gasquet. He had died on that mountain. He had sent no messages. It had been Madame Dubois all along.

"Why, madame?" I asked, widening my stance, relaxing my arms, quieting my breath. I was only a few feet from her. Close enough to act if a distraction presented itself. Close enough to see the pale blue eyes were not the serene eyes of Sister MJ, not the pleading mother's eyes of Madame Dubois, but the eyes of a madwoman.

"Where is René?" I asked, sinking further into a position of soft balance, preparing my long legs to act.

"He's been following you. René!" she called. There was a rustle in the undergrowth. Out stepped René holding a knife at Jorn's throat. Jorn and I looked at each other. So much for *our* surprise attack.

Jorn said, "Told you to stop for coffee."

I shook my head in disgust and turned back to Madame Dubois. "Madame, what is this all about?"

She nodded at Jorn. "He's to blame. He came home, and my son did not."

"He was wounded."

"Did he go back for my son? Did he search for him? *Non*." She held the gun steady, expertly.

"What do you want?" I asked.

"I want him to pay."

"How is shooting my mother revenge for Gasquet?" I cried.

"She was an accident." Madame Dubois dismissed Evie with a lift of one shoulder. "I wanted it to be you. I wanted Jorn to hold your dead body and know it was his fault, know that he had killed you just like he killed my Gasquet." Her eyes grew more turbulent. "I wanted him to feel the pain I feel every day, every hour, every second! I wanted him to suffer!" I'd never heard such hatred dripping from a voice.

Jorn spoke, wincing as René pressed the knife harder against his throat, drawing a trickle of blood. "Madame, I would do anything to bring back Gasquet. You must believe me. He was my best friend."

"It is dangerous to be your friend, Monsieur Jorn," she said.

As she lifted the gun higher, toward me, taking a breath

to steady her aim, I knew I couldn't wait. And so did Jorn. From the corner of my vision, I saw him jam an elbow into René's gut, shove the knife away, and fall to his knees. Caught off guard, René shouted and dropped the knife. Suddenly, he and Jorn were rolling on the ground, wrestling for control in the leaves and dirt.

Madame Dubois screamed, "René!" and, just at that moment, when her eyes shifted to her son, I struck. I took a step closer and swept my leg up, knocking the gun from her hand. It fired, wide, as it fell to the ground. I dove for the gun. When I had it firmly in hand, I rolled to my knees and turned toward Madame Dubois in time to catch a glimpse of madame's ivory jacket disappearing into the woods. She was escaping.

Jorn and René were still struggling, so I ran after Gasquet's mother. I could hear her ahead of me, crashing through the brush, snapping branches. I was younger and in shape; she didn't have a chance, I thought, but then a golden blur passed me. And a scream echoed through the trees. I put on speed, rounded a curve in the path, and skidded to a stop.

There was Madame Dubois. On her back, on the ground, locked in a staring contest with Darling the cheetah. Muzzle lowered within snapping distance of Madame Dubois's neck, Darling had the woman pinned. Madame Dubois's eyes were wide with terror; she barely breathed.

Darling purred, which in cheetah can mean anything from contentment to watch out.

I heard running steps behind me and spun around. It was Paulette. She came up in a skinny lope, wheezing.

"I gotta stop smoking," she panted, folding at the waist.

"Call Darling off, Paulette," I said.

Still panting, she groaned, "And spoil her fun?"

"Please."

"Oh, all right." Paulette straightened and slapped her thigh. "Here, Darlin'. Leave that lady alone."

Darling raised her head, looked back at Paulette, then leaped off Madame Dubois and casually walked over to Paulette's side. The cat's head butted Paulette's hip. Paulette praised her, "Good girl, good trackin'."

There was a rustle in the woods, a stumbling through the leaves, and Jorn appeared, a bruise on his cheek and his jacket torn. He pulled René by the arm into the clearing, and behind them walked a stranger. A darker shade than René, the man was older and exuded a distinguished air in a well-fitted suit and a starched white shirt. The resemblance was unmistakable though. This was Gasquet and René's father, Aristide Dubois.

Upon seeing her husband, Madame Dubois scrambled to her knees, her arms reaching for him. "Aristide! You have come to save me."

Walking to his wife and kneeling beside her, he said in a gentle voice with a thick accent, "Marie, what have you done?"

"I was attacked by this beast, and this woman!" Madame Dubois looked frail and confused, a smudge of dirt on her cheek, her silver hair in disarray, her elegant suit muddied and stained. Her husband pulled her into his arms.

Our chase and the appearance of Darling had sent the local wildlife scrambling for cover. But now, into the silent clearing swept a large crow. It landed and hopped along a branch above Madame Dubois's head. We stared at each other, and I remembered the crow outside Evie's room. Evie. Lying in a bed, perhaps never to wake. Larry lost beyond finding without his soul mate. It was unbearable to imagine. The fire that had been growing inside my soul burst into a rush of grief and such pain that I almost doubled with it. And before I realized it, I was stepping into the dark, into an alley of no return: feeling the heaviness of the gun in my hand, seeing my hand rise.

I pointed the gun at Madame Dubois.

CHAPTER 30

TO HECK
WITH AHIMSA

M AYA!" JORN SHOUTED.

Not sparing a glance for him, I said, "She shot Evie."

"Don't do this, Maya," Jorn begged.

Aristide said not a word, just protectively pushed Madame Dubois behind him. He knelt in the leaves, his chest square, his head lifted, watching me.

"No!" René cried, struggling in Jorn's hold.

"Uh, Maya, you know how to use that thing?" asked Paulette.

I ignored all of them. I stared at Madame Dubois peeking from behind her husband and images flooded my mind:

Sister MJ praying and pretending to care at Evie's bedside; Larry, more broken than I had ever seen him; Sadie shouting, "Well, *somebody* has to do something." And the fury raced cheetah-fast through me, squelching the compassion I had been taught at my mother's side and at Whispering Spirit from a reformed Hell's Angel.

Guilt and pain and anger were a festering stew inside me, and my heart was breaking for what I was about to do.

"Give me a reason to love you," I begged.

Because only love could save me. I knew that deep down, where all that I believed existed, where I fought to live the principle of *ahimsa* and to harm no creature, where I battled for my inner peace every day. I knew love could pull me back from the edge. If only I could find it, remember it. I had never felt this vacuum of compassion before. This emptiness, this lack of feeling for another human being, frightened me like nothing ever had.

From somewhere in the inner caverns of the soul came a thought: What would Evie think?

And then the void began to crack.

The crow tapped at the tree limb for my attention.

Paulette's voice stirred the air back to life with a lazy drawl. "Love don't need a reason, sugar."

Jorn begged, "Maya, it's over. Think about what you're doing. Please."

Paulette, who held no truck with sentimentality, said, "If you're gonna shoot her, shoot her."

I looked over at the woman who had done more to raise my mother than anyone else. She was calmly pulling a cigarette from the fanny pack at her toothpick waist. I could imagine that voice guiding a young Evie in the dark of night when she was scared and unsure, when she was filled with so much anger and pain that she didn't know herself.

"But don't do it for Evie," she said, lighting the cigarette, blowing a stream of smoke into the air, and looking me in the eye. "Don't lay it at her door. Do it for you."

The crow above Madame Dubois fluttered its wings, cawed, and settled. A breeze broke through the thick woods into the clearing and lifted my hair. My hand began to tremble as a thought slammed into me: you cannot go home if you lose your soul.

In the cool breeze on my cheek, in the voice of the crow, I heard Tum: "Walk away, Maya. Let it be."

In the chambers of my heart, I heard Evie, "No one can take your soul, Maya. You can only give it."

And that wasn't happening today.

I lowered the gun.

Jorn released René and rushed over to me. He carefully took the heavy weapon from my hand and stuffed it in the waistband of his jeans, then he slid his arm around me and held me. Everyone took a breath. Aristide slowly helped Madame Dubois to her feet.

I looked at René. Two crows. Mirrored images. I said, "It was you at the museum, the hospital, the florist."

René searched his mother's face, looking for direction, but her eyes were unfocused, her fingers running up and down the chain at her neck like worry beads.

Aristide frowned. "René, have you been masquerading as your brother?"

René's head dropped. "Yes, *Papa*."

"Explain."

The order was not to be defied. This was a man who was not easily ignored. I thought of Gasquet, how difficult it must have been to refuse Aristide with his commanding presence, how much courage it had taken Gasquet to set off on his own path. René was not as strong as his older brother.

The story poured out quickly: Madame Dubois wanted Jorn to pay for the death of her son, and René wanted to return the Mourner to the family vault and earn his mother's approval. So, he and his mother had conceived a plot of revenge.

"The Mourner has always been in our family, and Gasquet stole it!" René cried, as if that were an excuse.

Aristide shook his head in sadness. "René, René, your brother did not steal the Mourner. I gave it to him."

That shocked the young Dubois. "What?"

"When I realized I could not keep Gasquet close to home, that I could not stop him from going off into this dangerous world, I hoped a part of the family history would tether him to us. I wanted to remind him of one's loyalty to family. I hoped one day it would bring him back to us. He was a Dubois, after all."

"Then why did Gasquet's lawyers send our family heirloom to *him*?" René looked at Jorn with disgust. Someone at the law offices in Paris must have broken his vow of confidentiality. It had been René, who had tried to break into Jorn's house.

Aristide lifted an eyebrow in question to Jorn. "You have the Mourner?"

"Yes, monsieur," said Jorn. "I've been wondering what to

do with it. Now I know. I'm giving it back to the museum, monsieur."

"You can't do that," René objected. "It's ours."

Ignoring René and holding Aristide's steady gaze, Jorn said, "It's what Gasquet would have wanted."

Aristide considered Jorn for a moment then nodded. "*C'est vrai.* Gasquet, my difficult son." His voice, filled with love, caught. "This is what we get for teaching our children to search for beauty in this world."

"That was the Gasquet I knew," Jorn said. "That's why these mysterious messages, the shooting of Evie, never fit. He was a good man."

"*Oui*," Aristide said.

Jorn's arm around my waist tensed. "I'm so sorry your son died on that mountainside so far from home and family, monsieur. I'm sorry he died alone."

Madame Dubois roused and pointed a shaking finger at Jorn. "Liar!" she screamed. "You killed my son. God told me so." She turned desperate eyes to her husband. "Aristide, God told me so."

René immediately ran to his mother's side, tried to comfort her. "*Maman*, it is all right," René crooned, patting her shoulder.

Aristide cupped his wife's face in his palms. "The video was a lie, Marie. A horrible lie. Hush, now."

"Video?" Jorn's face froze with shock.

Aristide took a breath, gently cradled his wife's head to his chest, and looked at Jorn. "We received a demand for ransom for Gasquet, not long after you both were ambushed. His captors claimed to have found Gasquet wounded and had nursed him back to health. They sent us his cell phone as proof."

So, that was how René and Madame Dubois sent the text messages.

"They demanded a large sum of money for his release," Aristide said, his voice tired. "We paid. But Gasquet was never returned to us. Instead, we received a video—"

René took a step toward Jorn, his fists clenched by his side. "They cut off his head." He spat the words at Jorn. "You bastard, you left him there with those animals."

Jorn fell back a step, reeling.

Darling moaned, and Paulette placed a hand on the cat's head to comfort her.

I reached out for Jorn, my hand finding air. He shook his head again and again, backing away from me. "No, no, no."

I stepped up to him, grabbed the lapels of his jacket, and shook him. "Not. Your. Fault."

"He deserves to suffer, like my Gasquet!" Madame Dubois shouted, beating on her husband's chest with her fists, demanding he bring her justice.

Aristide rocked his wife. "*Non*, Marie, the video was a fake."

René spun toward his father. "Fake? Impossible."

"I took it to experts, René. They are sure Gasquet was already dead when the video was made. The captors lied to us. They found his body, recognized him, knew we had wealth, and used him as a prop to extort money."

I saw the weight of weeks of uncertainty fall from Jorn's tired shoulders. It was over. His friend was truly gone, murdered by child soldiers on a mountain road, children that Gasquet would have probably photographed with compassion to show the world what terrible things we do to our young. I took in the scene, Aristide comforting his wife; René studying the ground, a lost expression on his face; Paulette standing to the side in silence. Overhead, the crow stretched its neck and watched me.

Slowly, Jorn approached Madame Dubois. He lifted Gasquet's St. Joseph medal from his neck and offered it to Gasquet's mother. Pausing as he searched for words, Jorn finally said, "Gasquet loved to sing." He gave her a gentle smile. "But he had a terrible voice."

Madame Dubois unclenched one hand that had been caught against her husband's chest and tentatively reached for the medal. She folded it into her palm like a precious egg and sniffed, tears sliding down her cheeks.

"*Oui*," she whispered.

Jorn went on, "He thought all his jokes were funny."

Madame Dubois's lips curved into the suggestion of a smile, her eyes still on the medal in her palm.

Jorn continued. "He drove me crazy with his need to organize everything, even the food on his plate. And—and he smiled like an angel."

Madame Dubois looked up at Jorn then, her gaze hungry for more, more gifts of memories of the son she would never hold again. The eyes of a madwoman were gone, leaving only those of a grieving mother.

We followed Aristide, Madame Dubois, and René out of the woods. Aristide kept his wife tucked close to his side, helping her over ground that she had fleetingly conquered only shortly before. They had aged since they entered these woods. Perhaps we all had.

CHAPTER 31

LOVE CAN
UNHINGE US ALL

T*HIS IS WHAT I know,* I wrote in the Down Dog Diary, *always take note of a person's shoes. They'll tell you where she's been, what her world is like, what she's up to next—and whether you'll be running for your life any minute.*

Evie came back to life—on the day I nearly took Madame Dubois's. Paulette and Gran were there by her side. As Paulette explained it, Evie just opened her eyes, looked straight at her, and said with great difficulty, "Maya. Church. Go." Those were her first words. They never questioned how my mother knew I was in trouble. When my mom takes that tone of voice, even Paulette doesn't hesitate. Paulette immediately turned to Larry and asked what church Evie could be talking about, but he was no help. Gran said it had to be the chapel with the tent revival and insisted she would come along to find me, until Paulette told her, "I travel light and with a big cat." So, my mother sent Paulette, who drove like she did on the back roads of Texas as a kid, as if a rhumba of rattlesnakes were on her tail.

That was a month ago. Grandmother was still here. At this very moment, she and Evie were sitting in the garden amid the purple fall asters, Gran in Chanel as usual and Evie in her paint shirt. Gran was probably praying, and Evie, her hair still unbearably short from the surgery, had her face tilted up to the fading sun, eyes closed. Larry was in his office up to his high tops in programming a new game.

When we brought Evie home from the hospital, we didn't know how much of the old Evie would come back to us. We'd been warned by Evie's caregivers of possible personality changes and emotional instability. We'd had no idea if Evie would take up painting again after the brain injury, if her signature calm would be replaced by fits of temper, if she would enjoy the same foods or the same kinds of books. The doctor had warned us to be patient.

Since the shooting and her recovery, Evie tends to forget things. Words slip away like leaves on the autumn wind. This confuses Evie but doesn't seem to frighten or dishearten her. It hurts us, though, to see her at these times, but in typical Evie fashion, she simply shrugs, laughs, and goes on to something else. She is teaching us to live in the moment.

I sense a chink in my strong mother's armor, a vulnerability that wasn't there before, and I desperately want to patch it. But it is not a problem I can fix. Even though Evie is home, none of us is breathing normally yet. Heart's snap has a little less bite. The vibes around Larry and Gran aren't as tense, and Sadie visits Evie every chance she gets. Both seem to find comfort in gathering the coloring books and crayons and spending hours in colorful concentration at the kitchen table. As for me, my eyes tear up at the smallest things. Maybe I have what Val has, PTSD.

When the doorbell rang, I closed the diary.

It was Jorn. Without a hello, he walked in. "I still can't believe it," he said, following me back through the house to the studio window that overlooked the backyard, the portal to Evie's garden world. I watched my mother, almost afraid to take my eyes from her. Jorn spotted Evie in the garden and nodded toward her. "She's letting them get away with it. And you're helping her."

"Yes," I said.

Evie had decided she wanted no part in the prosecution of Madame Dubois. Jorn and I were fairly sure it was Madame Dubois, and not René, who had pulled the trigger. Aristide had confided that neither of his sons had ever taken to the firing range, but their mother was another story.

Aristide turned out to be much like Gasquet had depicted him to Jorn: strong-minded and opinionated. But I also found him fair and a determined protector of his family. He liked his own way, but who of us didn't? He had been in Japan on business when he came home to find his wife and son gone on an unexpected trip to America. He'd grown suspicious when he learned Madame Dubois was appearing as Sister MJ in a small town in Minnesota, the town where Peter Jorn lived. Aristide had been worried about his wife's mental condition for some time. Some days her grief overwhelmed her, and she did not have the strength to eat or talk or even pray. At other times, she rambled incessantly, fixated on Jorn and how he'd left their son to die. Aristide had thought eventually she would come to grips with the loss of their first born; he never dreamed the situation would turn to violence.

But as the woman said on that day we watched a heart-broken girl fling her ex's footgear from the rooftop, "Love can unhinge us all." It almost did me, and I had no doubt it had unbalanced the mind of Madame Dubois long ago.

After some discussion and much apologizing, Aristide took Madame Dubois back to Paris, promising she would get the best psychiatric care. Sister MJ did not finish the tent revival and, according to her website, had taken an extended leave of absence from future appearances.

"The outcome of this case is not Evie's decision," Jorn said. "Laws were broken."

The investigator who came to visit us said the same thing. The authorities had been brought in, he said; a shooting is a matter for the law. But Evie and I refused to cooperate or give a statement. Neither one of us mentioned the Duboises in connection with the shooting. Evie said she didn't remember anything about the evening she was shot, not even our walk around the lake, which was true. And I, knowing Evie's wishes regarding the Dubois family, maintained that I didn't know anything either.

The investigator didn't believe me. He had the selfie that Heart had insisted we turn in, and he had talked to the Dubois family, who maintained that they did not know the whereabouts of Gasquet. Which was true. His body was never recovered.

"If we catch this guy, the prosecutor will convene a grand jury," the investigator told me. "You'll be forced to testify about what you know. If you don't, they can throw you in jail for contempt."

"That sounds like an awful lot of effort just to learn what I've already told you," I said. "I don't know anything."

The investigator was stuck. There were no witnesses, and he didn't have a weapon.

Jorn heaved a sigh as he watched the two women in the garden. "So what did you do with the gun?"

"Gun?" I asked innocently.

He turned, shifted to lean a shoulder against the window jamb, and considered me. "Madame Dubois's gun. You and I both know it was used to shoot your mother. It was in my Jeep with René's knife. Where are they?"

"I actually don't know where they are at this very moment," I said.

Jorn's eyes narrowed.

In all the rush and joy of welcoming Evie back to the living, no one noticed when I slipped out of Evie's crowded hospital room, went down to the parking garage, and removed the weapons from Jorn's Jeep. At that time, I didn't know what I was going to do with them; I was just following my intuition. But later that night, after watching Paulette with Evie, how she whispered to Evie as she tucked the blankets protectively closer, how she made Evie smile with her promise to help my mother "put on her face so she didn't look half-dead," I hatched a plan.

After wiping down the gun and knife to remove fingerprints—mine, Jorn's, Madame Dubois's, and René's—I wrapped the gun and knife in a heavy cloth sack and gave the sack to Paulette. Without a word exchanged, she understood immediately what I wanted her to do. Somewhere on her way back to New York, likely on a bridge in the middle of the night, she and Pavel would pull over, and, without ever looking in the sack or asking what it contained, they would drop it into a deep river.

"Is this the way things are handled in Whispering Spirit?" Jorn asked.

I just smiled at him.

We each had our ways of managing what cannot be managed. Jorn had returned the Mourner to the Musée des Beaux-Arts de Dijon in France. It was done anonymously and with Aristide Dubois's agreement. It was a story Jorn would never write, a truth that would never be told. Just like Evie's story.

When he realized he wasn't getting any more explanations from me, Jorn let go of his exasperation and walked over to a painting on an easel. It was Evie's latest, a field of sunflowers, densely packed, a curtain so bright and yellow that they nearly hurt the eye. Jorn wrinkled his nose and said, "It's not quite right, is it?"

I joined Jorn and considered the painting.

"Remember the day Val crashed the yoga class?" I asked. "We were practicing Warrior Poses."

"Who could forget?" Jorn rolled his shoulder in memory.

"In the story of Shiva and Sati, Shiva realizes he was wrong to take revenge on the king. It did not bring back his beloved Sati. He leaves his mountain and revives Sati's father, replacing his head. He chooses forgiveness."

"Just like Evie," Jorn said.

I thought for a moment. Maybe "chooses" was the wrong word. Shiva *became* forgiveness.

Shiva let it be.

Why do we resort to violence to heal our fears? Shiva had feared what Madame Dubois had feared and what, in the end, I had feared—a life without the person we each loved. I had a long way to go. I had yet to forgive Madame Dubois. I was no Shiva.

In companionable silence, I stood beside Jorn in front of Evie's painting. Finally, Jorn spoke, "There's definitely something creepy about this painting. It's too—nice."

I knew what Jorn meant. Evie's work always carried a bite—flowers that devoured, animals that plotted and connived. And there was always ambiguity, an escape hatch to be used or not, depending on the viewer's perspective. This, like all her work since the shooting, seemed to be missing Evie's edgy, subliminal message of unease with a world she still stubbornly trusted. Had the injury somehow changed her perceptions? Where was our old Evie? She had to be in there somewhere. I closed my eyes and opened them again, softening my vision like one does in those optical games. My mother's spirit was there; I just wasn't seeing it.

And then I found it. "There," I pointed.

Jorn leaned closer until his nose was practically touching the painting. "Shoes?"

Amid the tall sunflower stalks were two chubby legs and baby toes peeking from a grubby pair of sandals. A child in the field of sunflowers. You could believe she was play-fully hiding. You could believe she was trapped in a land of menacing flora. But, if you looked really close, you could see one small foot pointed away from the other, indicating the thought of freedom and the ability to escape. I smiled.

Evie was back.

ACKNOWLEDGMENTS

BOOKS HAVE MAGIC, and readers hold the key to unlocking the spells that keep us turning the pages long into the night, that make us laugh or cry, that make us feel less alone. I am eternally grateful to my readers, for those who love stories and words as much as I do.

I also would like to thank friends who have so generously given me their time, attention, and wisdom while writing this book: Marlys Dooley, Lois West Duffy, Miriam Karmel, Janet Hanafin, Jean Housh, Ann Woodbeck, and the wonderful Faith Sullivan. You are my most excellent mentors and guides. I am so fortunate to have you.

Thank you as well to others who have answered questions, read early drafts, and helped me see more clearly the path I needed to take: Emmalynn Bauer and the Minneapolis Institute of Art, Cathy Bucholz, Tom Combs, Allen Eskens, Neal Ewers, Timya Owen, and Geanette Poole.

My thanks to Kathey Amaral, Cathleen Tarawhiti, Monique Wanner, and Greg Mimbs for contributing to a stunning cover.

To Sarah Roberts Delacueva, one of my insightful

editors, you give me your time and talent when I know it is not always convenient as the mother of a two-year-old. Your observations, catches, and suggestions never steer me wrong. And your love always warms me.

To Suzanne Roberts, you bring light, love, and energy when I most need it. I adore every moment that we share.

Finally, and most importantly, thank you to Tony Roberts. Because of you, I am always striving to be a better writer. You inspire me to reach higher, go longer, and never give up—whether I'm on a mountain hiking trail or I'm struggling to be the writer I want to be. Keep pushing me, my friend.

ABOUT THE AUTHOR

SHERRY ROBERTS is the author of award-winning mysteries and literary fiction. *Down Dog Diary* and *Warrior's Revenge* are part of the Maya Skye novels. *Book of Mercy* is a funny novel about a serious issue: censorship, *Maud's House* is a story of lost-and-found creativity, and *WriteTips* is a guide to giving your writing power and improving your business.

She has contributed essays and articles to national publications and anthologies including *USA Today* and the *Saint Paul Almanac*. Her short fiction has been published in newspapers, literary magazines, and *O. Henry Literary Festival Short Stories*.

She lives in Apple Valley, Minnesota, where she feeds the hummingbirds, rides her bike, reads by the fire, bakes cookies, and practices yoga and tai chi.

Visit Sherry's website at sherry-roberts.com.

WHAT'S NEXT?

SIGN UP FOR SHERRY'S EMAIL LIST (sherry-roberts.com) for updates on future writing—plus get free books, short stories, or other offers available only to fans! Your email will never be shared, you can unsubscribe at any time, and Sherry promises not to paper your inbox with emails.

Also follow Sherry Roberts Author on Facebook to get the latest on her books and writing in general.

LEAVE A REVIEW. If you enjoyed this book, please consider leaving a brief review on Goodreads, Amazon, or other retailer site. Readers spreading the word to other readers is invaluable to authors and their work. If you're shy, just drop me a line on the contact page of sherry-roberts.com. Your support and ideas are important to me. I promise I'll write back.

CHECK OUT MY OTHER BOOKS. In Maya Skye's first adventure, *Down Dog Diary*, she goes up against killers to protect a mysterious diary. In *Book of Mercy*, a dyslexic woman takes on a town banning books. If you love art and creativity, give *Maud's House* a try. All of my books are available in paperback and eBook at sherry-roberts.com, Amazon, and other retail outlets. If you can't find my books in your local bookstore, ask for them. Ask your local library to carry my books.

www.ingramcontent.com/pod-product-compliance
Lightning Source LLC
Chambersburg PA
CBHW020613110726
47899CB00002B/490